THE FLOWER COTTAGE

A SWEET SMALL TOWN ROMANCE

THE COTTAGES ON ANCHOR LANE, BOOK 1

LEEANNA MORGAN

D1521619

WELCOME TO SAPPHIRE BAY!

Nestled against the shore of Flathead Lake, Montana, you'll find the imaginary town of Sapphire Bay.

Here you'll discover a community with big hearts, warm smiles, and lots of wonderful stories to be told. Romance, adventure, and intrigue are all waiting for you! Let's explore Sapphire Bay together in *The Flower Cottage*, the first book in the 'Cottages on Anchor Lane' series.

Fans of Robyn Carr's Virgin River series will love this small-town, feel-good romance!

Paris Haynes has spent most of her life running from one bad relationship to the next. Three years ago, determined to put her past behind her, she moved to Sapphire Bay and began to rebuild her life.

Working with Kylie in the flower shop has given her a sense of purpose, a reason to live the kind of life she's always dreamed about. When she hears about the cottages that are being remodeled on Anchor Lane, she can hardly contain her excitement. She proposes a plan so outrageous, so out of her comfort zone, that she's sure it will fail before it begins.

Richard Dawkins lost his leg in Afghanistan and nearly lost his son. Moving to Sapphire Bay has given him more than a place to call home. He has new friends, a steady job, and a state-of-the-art prosthetic leg that's transformed his life.

Helping to turn the cottages on Anchor Lane into small, thriving businesses is his way of giving back to the community. But when he discovers Paris has been given the keys to the first cottage, he knows he's in trouble. With her over-the-top positivity, she's everything he doesn't need, and the only person who could change his life forever.

THE FLOWER COTTAGE is the first book in 'The Cottages on Anchor Lane' series and can easily be read as a stand-alone. All of Leeanna's series are linked. If you find a character you like, they could be in another novel. Happy reading!

If you would like to know when Leeanna's next book is released, please visit leeannamorgan.com and sign up for my newsletter. Happy reading!

Other Novels by Leeanna Morgan:

Montana Brides:
Book 1: Forever Dreams (Gracie and Trent)
Book 2: Forever in Love (Amy and Nathan)
Book 3: Forever After (Nicky and Sam)
Book 4: Forever Wishes (Erin and Jake)
Book 5: Forever Santa (A Montana Brides Christmas Novella)
Book 6: Forever Cowboy (Emily and Alex)
Book 7: Forever Together (Kate and Dan)
Book 8: Forever and a Day (Sarah and Jordan)
Montana Brides Boxed Set: Books 1-3
Montana Brides Boxed Set: Books 4-6

The Bridesmaids Club:
Book 1: All of Me (Tess and Logan)
Book 2: Loving You (Annie and Dylan)
Book 3: Head Over Heels (Sally and Todd)
Book 4: Sweet on You (Molly and Jacob)
The Bridesmaids Club: Books 1-3

Emerald Lake Billionaires:
Book 1: Sealed with a Kiss (Rachel and John)
Book 2: Playing for Keeps (Sophie and Ryan)
Book 3: Crazy Love (Holly and Daniel)

Book 4: One And Only (Elizabeth and Blake)
Emerald Lake Billionaires: Books 1-3

The Protectors:
Book 1: Safe Haven (Hayley and Tank)
Book 2: Just Breathe (Kelly and Tanner)
Book 3: Always (Mallory and Grant)
Book 4: The Promise (Ashley and Matthew)
The Protectors Boxed Set: Books 1-3

Montana Promises:
Book 1: Coming Home (Mia and Stan)
Book 2: The Gift (Hannah and Brett)
Book 3: The Wish (Claire and Jason)
Book 4: Country Love (Becky and Sean)
Montana Promises Boxed Set: Books 1-3

Sapphire Bay:
Book 1: Falling For You (Natalie and Gabe)
Book 2: Once In A Lifetime (Sam and Caleb)
Book 3: A Christmas Wish (Megan and William)
Book 4: Before Today (Brooke and Levi)
Book 5: The Sweetest Thing (Cassie and Noah)
Book 6: Sweet Surrender (Willow and Zac)
Sapphire Bay Boxed Set: Books 1-3
Sapphire Bay Boxed Set: Books 4-6

Santa's Secret Helpers:
Book 1: Christmas On Main Street (Emma and Jack)
Book 2: Mistletoe Madness (Kylie and Ben)
Book 3: Silver Bells (Bailey and Steven)
Book 4: The Santa Express (Shelley and John)
Book 5: Endless Love (The Jones Family)
Santa's Secret Helpers Boxed Set: Books 1-3

CHAPTER 1

*P*aris placed a bouquet of pale pink roses into the refrigerator at Blooming Lovely, the only flower shop in Sapphire Bay. Three years after she'd started working with Kylie and Jackie, she still had to pinch herself to remember this wasn't a dream.

Before she'd arrived in Montana, her life was a complete mess. Now, with a little help from her friends, she finally felt as though she belonged in this small, amazing town.

"I've closed the store and put the cash into the safe. Is there anything else we need to do?" Jackie asked.

Paris opened the spreadsheet showing tomorrow's orders. "Other than printing off a list of the flowers I need from the market, we're finished for the day. Did Mrs. Smith tell you when she wants to collect her daughter's bouquet?"

"She'll be here as soon as we open."

"That's good. Have you heard from Kylie?"

"Not yet, but she should be here soon. I'll make us a hot drink while we wait."

Their boss, Kylie, was halfway through her first pregnancy and everyone was excited. This afternoon, she'd had an appointment at the medical clinic for a routine scan.

Paris checked her watch. Tomorrow morning, she was driving to Polson to re-stock their flowers. It was her favorite thing to do, even if she had to leave before sunrise to secure the best blooms.

"Sorry I'm late," Kylie said as she hurried through the back door. "Ben wanted to show Charlotte the scan of her baby sister."

"You're having a girl!" Paris left the list on the work table and hugged Kylie. "That's so exciting."

"Just think of all the cute outfits you can dress her in," Jackie said as she gave her boss another hug. "Was everything all right?"

"We're growing a healthy little girl. The only thing I need to watch is my blood pressure. The doctor wants me to work fewer hours for the rest of my pregnancy."

That didn't surprise Paris. Kylie worked long hours and hardly ever took a day off. "Jackie and I can spend more time here."

Kylie sat at their workroom table. "I'm not sure that will help." Gratefully, she took the cup Jackie handed to her.

"It's the special blend of berry tea you like."

"Thanks. It smells delicious." Taking a small sip, she sighed. "This is exactly what I need. While we were waiting for Charlotte, I looked at our bookings for the next six months. I don't know what I was thinking when I agreed to provide the flowers for so many events."

Paris sat beside her. "You have a successful business. Everyone wants Blooming Lovely to make floral arrangements for their special occasions."

"And our prices are much better than any of the florists in Polson." Jackie left a cup of coffee on the table for Paris before pulling out a stool for herself. "I looked at some websites the other day. I was shocked at what other florists are charging."

Kylie wrapped her hands around her cup. "They might have higher costs they need to cover. If I didn't own this store, I'd have to charge more, too."

"Well, I'm glad we can keep the prices of our flowers affordable. Without the extra business it's created, you might not have asked Paris and me to help you."

Paris frowned. "Are you thinking of canceling some of the events we've booked?"

"It's one option," Kylie said slowly. "Between Blooming Lovely and what you do for the Christmas Shop, neither of you have much free time. We'll be okay for the next few months. But, after that, I might have to give up work completely. Unless I can find another florist, we'll have to cancel some bookings or ask another company to provide the flowers."

Paris understood why her boss felt that way, but asking another company to work with their clients seemed like a giant step backward. "What if our customers don't come back? They could ask the new company to provide the flowers for other events they're hosting."

"That's a risk I'll have to take. I'm really sorry I can't work as many hours as we need."

"Don't be silly," Jackie said. "Your health is more important than anything else."

Paris thought about the people whose events would be affected if Kylie wasn't here to help. Even choosing which events to cancel would be difficult—especially in a small town where everyone knew each other.

Kylie left her cup on the table. "Would you like to see the ultrasound photos of our baby?"

With an excited nod, Jackie moved closer. "Can you tell who she looks like?"

"Ben said she has my nose and chin, but I have no idea why he thinks that."

Paris stood beside her two best friends and studied the images. She smiled when she realized what the baby was doing. "Is she sucking her thumb?"

"She is," Kylie placed her hand on her baby bump. "I can't wait to meet her. She was jumping around like a jellybean during the scan."

"She can't sit still, just like her mom," Jackie said with a grin. "You have a beautiful baby girl."

"And two friends who are happy to babysit whenever you need a break," Paris added. "Don't worry about the events we've booked. We'll find a way to get through the next few months."

"I hope so." Kylie looked sadly at Paris and Jackie. "I didn't think I'd have to cut back my hours."

"It's only for a little while." Paris gave Kylie another hug. "We're a team. We'll make it work."

As they admired the pictures of Kylie and Ben's baby, Paris knew everything would be okay. Kylie had worked hard to build Blooming Lovely into a successful business. Their clients would understand if they had to find another florist to make their bouquets and flower arrangements— especially when a new baby was involved.

RICHARD PARKED his truck outside The Welcome Center and rubbed his right leg. After a long day at work, he was glad to almost be home.

Looking across the parking lot, he smiled at the ocean-themed mural he'd created with his son. Before they'd joined the painting project, a row of uninspiring concrete garages separated The Welcome Center from the tiny home village. Working with the village's residents, they'd brought color and life to this side of the property.

The sense of belonging the project gave him was a stark contrast to how he'd felt when he arrived in Sapphire Bay. Emotionally and physically broken after his time in the army, he'd traveled here with his son, four suitcases, and a life that was the complete opposite of everything he'd imagined.

"Good afternoon, Mr. Dawkins."

Richard sighed. Only one person called him Mr. Dawkins, and he tried to stay away from her. Not that he'd had much luck. Sapphire Bay was so small that it was impossible to hide from anyone.

His eyebrows rose when he saw what Paris was wearing. "Let me guess. You're going for a 1950s rockabilly look."

Placing her hands on her pink polka dot skirt, she twisted left and then right. The petticoats under the skirt swished back and forth. "You're getting better. I thought about wearing my Marilyn Munroe dress, but Jackie thought it might be too much."

After seeing some of the outfits she wore, he'd probably agree with Jackie. Paris was like a chameleon, wearing clothes that were as over-the-top as her personality. "Why did you want to dress like Marilyn Munroe?"

"I'm looking after Natalie's art class. We're studying pop culture."

He must have spent too much time around her because he knew exactly what she meant. "And Andy Warhol created a famous painting of Marilyn Munroe."

"Exactly. Are you visiting The Welcome Center or going to the tiny home village?"

"The Welcome Center. Jack's writing class has nearly finished."

Paris lifted the strap of her pink handbag onto her shoulder. "I'll walk with you."

He wasn't sure that was a good idea. Whenever he saw her, one of them usually said something that offended the other. They were better staying apart and saying as little to each other as possible.

"Is Jack enjoying the after-school writing class?"

Richard nodded. At least discussing his son was a safe, neutral topic. "He is. Katie's a great tutor."

"Have you read her latest children's book? It's amazing."

"I'm reading it to Jack at the moment. Why are you tutoring the students in Natalie's art class?"

"She had to fly to Washington, D.C. to open her next exhibition."

"Teaching her class is a lot different from working in the flower shop."

Paris frowned. "You don't think I can do it?"

He could have kicked himself. "I didn't say that."

"Of course, you didn't. But you were thinking it." In true Paris form, she lengthened her stride and stalked away from him.

Richard ran his hand around the back of his neck. He'd met Paris a year ago at a fundraiser for the tiny home village. When he'd spoken to her, warning bells had flashed inside his head. She'd asked too many questions, seen far too much of the man he didn't want to remember. Each time he met her, he tried to figure out why they rubbed each other the wrong way. And, each time, he came away with nothing.

But not being able to understand her wasn't an excuse to make her feel bad.

He caught up to her as she was about to enter the center. "The students are lucky to have you helping them."

"*Now* you say something nice."

"I was surprised you're tutoring the class, that's all."

Paris sighed. "You don't know anything about me, so why should it surprise you?"

He crossed his arms in front of his chest. Most people were intimidated by his height and size, but not Paris. She stood her ground, making up for the difference in their builds by sheer personality. "I didn't know you could paint."

"I can't, but I did some art history papers at UCLA. Natalie wants her students to combine the screen-printing technique she showed them with a pop culture design. I'm supervising the class and answering their questions."

"That sounds interesting. I'm sure you'll do a great job."

"If that's an apology, thank you." She glanced at her watch. "I have to go. Otherwise, everyone will arrive before I do."

"And I'd better find Jack. He'll be wondering where I am."

In silence, they walked into the center and went their separate ways. As he waited with the other parents, he wondered what was wrong with him. With her sparkling blue eyes and jet-black hair, Paris was one of the most attractive women he'd ever met. Whenever he met someone who knew her, they described her as friendly and helpful. So, what was his problem?

"Dad!" Jack rushed out of a meeting room. "You're not going to believe what happened. Chandler vomited all over Mrs. Campbell. The smell was so bad we had to go to a different room."

"I hope Chandler's feeling better."

"He will be. Peggy-Anne said someone dared him to eat worms. Do you want to read my story when we get home?"

Richard took Jack's backpack out of his hands. "Sounds great." With his eight-year-old son chatting beside him, he followed the other parents into the foyer. The flash of a bright pink skirt farther down the corridor caught his eye. His heart sank.

He was tired, hungry, and guilty of thinking the worst of a woman who'd never harmed anyone. He couldn't have started the evening off worse if he'd tried.

THE FOLLOWING MORNING, Paris carried a box of flowers into Blooming Lovely. "He's so annoying. Each time I meet him, he says something that makes my blood boil."

Jackie opened a box she'd already brought inside. "He could be insecure."

"I don't think so. Richard's built like a big, bushy lumberjack, and he's taller than most men in Sapphire Bay. *And* he's a construction foreman at the old steamboat museum."

"Even big men have issues."

Carefully, Paris placed a dozen pale yellow roses on the counter. "As far as I can tell, the only issue he has, is with me."

Jackie grinned. "That would be a first. Our customers adore you, and Mr. Murray calls you his sweetheart."

"I don't mind what Mr. Murray calls me. He's ninety-four and thinks everyone's wonderful. Richard could learn a thing or two from him."

"You want your arch enemy to call you his sweetheart?"

"I'd sooner he didn't call me anything." She glanced at her watch and frowned. "We'd better bring the rest of the flowers inside. I need to make a special order before we open."

"And I promised Kylie I'd change the window display. I can't believe it's nearly Valentine's Day."

Neither could Paris. Each year seemed to go faster than the last. She looked around the workroom as they carried more boxes into Blooming Lovely. It was like an Aladdin's cave of gift-wrapping paper, glittery boxes, and flowers in all shapes and colors. "I don't know what I would have done if Kylie hadn't offered me this job."

"Neither do I, although I suspect Pastor John had a lot to do with us being here. Do you think Kylie will have to reduce our hours?"

Paris had wondered the same thing. "I asked her that yesterday. She doesn't think that will happen. All it will mean is we don't have to work seven days a week."

"I wouldn't want to be the person who tells our clients we can't provide the flowers for their special occasions."

"Neither would I." Paris opened the last box of flowers. "At least Valentine's Day won't be affected."

Jackie picked up a red rose and grinned. "Regardless of what Kylie does, Cupid will never stop creating happily ever afters in Sapphire Bay."

"As long as he stays away from me, he can do whatever he wants."

"For someone who loves Valentine's Day, that doesn't sound very romantic."

"I prefer to watch everyone else enjoy the day." Paris collected the paperwork from each box. "Can you hand me the list of orders we need to make?"

Jackie reached for the clipboard. "Just because you've had some horrible experiences with men, it doesn't mean they're all bad."

"That's what I used to tell myself, but it didn't make any difference. I have some kind of defect that makes me date the wrong people. I'm much happier on my own."

"I don't believe you."

Paris grinned. "You don't have to. Can you pass me the box beside you? I need the lilies for a bouquet."

"You can change the subject as often as you like but, one

day, you'll meet an amazing man who will sweep you off your feet."

Picking up a knife, Paris cut through the tape holding the box together. The likelihood of that happening was a million to one. Especially when her superpower was pushing people away.

CHAPTER 2

*R*ichard's heart pounded as he lay in bed, staring at the ceiling of his tiny home. He'd had another nightmare, the kind that left him drenched in sweat and lost somewhere between the streets of Kabul and a small town in rural Montana.

Taking a deep, shaky breath, he focused on the photo above him. Jack's smiling face pulled him away from the horror of losing his leg. The screams of his friends, the panic after the landmine destroyed more than one life. The dawning realization that he might never come home.

"Dad?" Jack's sleepy voice filled the space between the lofts.

"It's okay. Go back to sleep, buddy."

"Did you have a nightmare?"

Richard sat upright and pulled off his wet T-shirt. "I did, but I'm okay now."

"Do you need anything?"

Tears stung his eyes. His son was eight years old. He shouldn't have to babysit his dad and make sure he was okay after he broke down. "I'm all right. I'm sorry if I woke you."

Jack yawned. "I don't mind. Are you sure you're okay?"

"Positive. Goodnight, Jack."

"'Night, Dad."

He looked across the room. Jack's night-light cast a pale-yellow shadow on the wall, reminding him they were safe.

He used to pray the nightmares would end, that they'd disappear into the black hole he'd crawled out of so many times. But nothing, including two years of intense counseling, had banished them completely.

He rubbed the scars on his right thigh. Sometimes, on nights like this, he'd lie awake for hours, thinking about the well-meaning phrases that dripped off people's tongues. He knew he was lucky to be alive, lucky to have escaped the constant stress of not knowing if he'd ever see his parents and son again.

But knowing he was lucky meant nothing, when all he wanted to be was normal. He wanted to enjoy living with Jack and create furniture people were proud to own. It didn't seem like a lot to ask, but after the last eight years, even getting out of bed in the morning was a struggle.

Taking another deep breath, he glanced at where Jack was sleeping and reached for his earbuds. Hopefully, the music would send him into a dreamless sleep. If not, he'd open his laptop, design another piece of furniture, and wait for the sun to rise.

LATER THAT DAY, Richard stood in the entryway of the old cottage his construction crew were remodeling. Percy Adams, the Chairperson of the Heritage Protection Society, was telling him about the pressed tin ceiling.

Almost a year ago, Penny Terry, a local business owner and property developer, saw the eight cottages on Anchor

Lane and knew she could do something with them. After many meetings with the county, they were letting her create four small businesses and four community houses from the run-down cottages.

Built in the late nineteenth-century, they were originally vacation homes for the employees of the steamboat company in Polson. By the 1930s, when large-scale use of the steamboats was over, the cottages were abandoned. After they were gifted to the county, plans were made to repurpose them. But budget constraints and staff changes meant they remained empty for decades.

If Penny hadn't returned to Sapphire Bay after her grandmother died, the cottages would still be falling apart.

"Steel wool should remove most of the rust," Percy murmured as he studied the ceiling. "If that doesn't work, use a buffing attachment on a high-powered drill, but be careful. If you push too hard, you'll damage the tin."

"We'll go slowly."

"Did you buy the special primer I suggested?"

Taking a deep breath, Richard nodded. "I bought some last week." Since beginning the restoration project, Percy had made multiple visits to the cottages. His advice was always welcome but, sometimes, all Richard wanted was to get on with the remodeling.

A text pinged on his cell phone and he checked the message. "Do you have any more questions, Percy? I need to make a call."

"Do you know if Penny has found tenants for the cottages?"

"Not that she's told me. She should be here soon if you want to ask her."

"I'll talk to her later. Thanks for showing me around."

"You're welcome." There was no point in asking Percy to make an appointment for his next visit. He had a habit of dropping in unannounced and offering his suggestions on what they should be doing. The only positive thing about his visits was that he knew what he was talking about.

After Percy left, Richard called the person who'd texted him. With the shortage in building materials biting all construction projects hard, he'd ordered enough drywall for the first four cottages. Whether the supplier could get any was another story.

"Hi, Richard."

He turned around and frowned. Paris stood on the veranda wearing a blue and white gingham dress and bright red sneakers.

"Sorry," she whispered. "I didn't realize you were on the phone."

"It's okay. It's gone to voicemail." He ended the call and slipped the phone into his pocket. "Has anyone asked you where they can find the yellow brick road?"

Paris's eyes lit with laughter. "Not yet, but Mabel Terry took a photo of me for the community Facebook page. Is Penny here?"

"Not at the moment, but she should arrive soon."

Paris checked her watch. "Is it okay if I wait for her? She wants to talk to me about some flower arrangements."

"That's okay. But, if you stay, you'll need to wear a hard hat and sign our visitor's register." Reaching into the box beside the front door, he pulled out a bright red hat.

"It matches my sneakers."

He didn't know what to say. With the hard hat perched on her head, she looked even cuter than before. "The register is sitting on the table."

Paris looked at where he was pointing and picked up the pen. "It's like Fort Knox."

"If we don't follow the correct health and safety procedures, the county will shut down the construction site."

"And no one wants that." With a flourish, she signed her name and looked into the next room. "When I last saw this cottage, it was full of trash and cobwebs."

"A lot has changed since then."

"You can say that again. I admire what you're doing. Most people would have run a mile if they saw these buildings."

Richard wouldn't have blamed them. With rotten framing, water-damaged ceilings and walls, and a large population of rats and mice, they were everything a property developer didn't need. "It's just as well Penny saw past the years of neglect."

"She did an amazing job of remodeling the inn with her sisters. Would you mind if I look inside the cottage?"

"It's not a good time. A team of electricians are rewiring, and the plumbers are working in the bathroom and kitchen."

"I won't get in their way."

With her big blue eyes pleading at him, he was finding it hard to say no. "You can't wander around on your own."

"You could show me what you've done. It won't take long."

With a resigned sigh, he ignored the next call coming from his phone. "Don't touch anything and watch where you step."

"Yes, sir."

Richard frowned. Not that Paris was paying him any attention. Her eyes were focused on the ceiling.

"I haven't seen anything like this. It's gorgeous."

"It's made from pressed tin. Once we remove the rust it will be even better. The first door on your right is the former living room."

Paris stepped into the spacious room. After admiring the sash windows, she headed toward the fireplace. "Are you leaving this here?"

"We are. The tile surround isn't part of the original

design, but it looks good. The historical society thinks it was added in the 1920s."

"That makes sense. If I wanted an art deco fire surround, I'd use black and white tiles like these ones, too." Stepping around the electrician's ladder, she looked at the bare timber framing. "I didn't realize you were doing so much."

"We're taking the cottage back to its original framing. By doing that, we can insulate the walls, rewire everything, and replace the ancient plumbing."

Biting her bottom lip, Paris moved through the large opening they'd made in the wall connecting this room to the next.

He'd better explain what they were doing in case she thought the entire house was turning into one room. "Because the cottage will be used for a small business, we're opening up this side of the house. With some shelving and display cases, it will make a great showroom or open concept work area. The kitchen and bathroom are at the back of the cottage. They'll stay where they are. The front bedroom could be an office, a reception area, or a large storage room."

"It sounds perfect." Paris moved out of the way of an electrician. "Penny said you hoped to have the first cottage finished by mid-March."

"We've had a few issues with buying supplies, so that's pushed the completion date out by a couple of weeks."

"That's better than I thought. From the outside, they look as though they'll take a lot longer to remodel." After a quick survey of the kitchen and bathroom, Paris walked into the former front bedroom. "It will be amazing when it's finished."

"I hope so. It's an ideal location for a business."

Penny appeared in the doorway. "Sorry I'm late, Paris."

"That's okay. Richard has been showing me around the cottage. It looks great."

"I think so, too. All we need to do is find a tenant." Penny took a notepad out of her pocket. "Thanks for meeting me here. I thought it would make designing the floral arrangements easier if you saw the cottage."

"Tell me what you need."

Richard's cell phone rang. "I'd better answer this call."

"Thanks for showing me around," Paris said.

"You're welcome." And with his phone against his ear, he walked outside to discuss a missing order. It was a pity Paris couldn't click the heels of her red shoes to make their building supplies appear. If they couldn't find their drywall, the entire project would come to a standstill. And that would push the completion date into whenever.

PARIS ADDED a daisy to the bouquet she was making and glanced at Kylie. After leaving the cottage on Anchor Lane, she hadn't stopped thinking about what she could do with the remodeled building. Although it wasn't large, it had lots of street appeal and was in a perfect location to attract the tourists who came to town.

After spending most of the evening second-guessing herself, she'd come up with an idea so outrageous, so unlike her other harebrained ideas, that it could almost work.

She wasn't sure what her boss would think, but she had to ask. "I've been thinking about the cottages on Anchor Lane," she said to Kylie.

"I meant to ask how your appointment with Penny went."

"It was a good meeting. She knows what kind of flowers she wants, so that made everything a lot easier. But that's not what I was thinking about." Taking a deep breath, she focused on the idea that had kept her awake. "I have a business proposition for you. If you think I'm crazy, tell me."

Kylie smiled. "Okay, but crazy is the last word I'd use to describe you."

Crossing her fingers, Paris hoped she felt the same way after she'd heard her idea. "While I was walking through the cottage, I thought about the number of clients we'll have to turn away when you're working fewer hours. What if there was another florist who specialized in providing flowers for large events and gifts for the Christmas shop? Blooming Lovely could focus on smaller events like birthday parties and wedding anniversaries, and provide flowers for people who haven't preordered anything."

"That could work, but there isn't another flower shop in Sapphire Bay."

"There might be. What if I opened my own store? We could work together to make sure we aren't taking customers away from each other. Hiring more staff won't be too difficult, either. A couple of people in the adult flower arranging class I'm tutoring would be perfect apprentices."

Kylie looked thoughtfully at the half-finished bouquet in front of her. "Before you worked with me, I only made flowers for smaller events. There was more than enough work to keep me busy and make a healthy profit. And, to be honest, I enjoy that side of my business more than decorating large events."

Paris breathed a sigh of relief. At least Kylie had listened to what she'd said. "You wouldn't need to worry about replacing me. Jackie is a wonderful florist and she wants full-time, permanent hours. She could teach an apprentice the basics."

"It sounds like a great idea, but do you really want to start your own business? It's a huge commitment."

"I know I can do it. I enjoy working with flowers and making people happy. You've taught me a lot about owning a business."

Kylie reached for another flower. "When you and Jackie started working here, I hoped you'd take what you learned and create something special for yourselves. I just didn't expect my pregnancy and this opportunity to happen at the same time."

Paris' heart sank. "I'll understand if you don't think it will work."

"I'm not saying that. Specializing in certain types of clients makes sense. Especially when the large events we decorate can take weeks to organize. Let me think about it."

"While you're doing that, I'll talk to Penny about leasing the first cottage."

"When do you want to open the new flower shop?"

"The cottage won't be ready until the middle of March, so it would be sometime after that."

Kylie nodded. "From my perspective, it's perfect timing. Have you spoken to Jackie about your idea?"

Paris shook her head. "I thought I'd speak to you first."

"That sounds sensible. Now, tell me about the flowers Penny wants for the opening of the cottage."

Paris told Kylie about the baskets of flowers Penny wanted for the veranda and the arrangement that would add color to the food table. In the back of her mind, she imagined what the store could look like as a flower shop. If Kylie was happy for her to proceed, it could be a dream come true.

CHAPTER 3

*E*ighteen months ago, walking along the shore of Flathead Lake with his son was impossible for Richard. Now, with the help of a state-of-the-art prosthetic leg, he could do everything he'd done before he was injured.

Jack leaped across the rocks, searching for more stones to skip across the water. In the distance, fishing boats bobbed up and down. Trout, bass, and whitefish lurked at the bottom of the lake, enticing locals and visitors onto the water. If that wasn't a good enough reason to come here, the stunning scenery and laidback lifestyle would do it.

"I've found some stones." Jack joined him on the boardwalk, opening his palm to show him his treasures.

"They look great. How many times will they skip?"

Jack picked up one of the stones and rubbed his thumb along its flat surface. "Five."

"Impressive." Taking one of the stones he'd found earlier out of his pocket, Richard tossed it in the air. "I'm thinking this one will make four."

With a laugh, Jack made his way to the edge of the water.

"Whoever does the most skips gets to choose the ice cream flavor we buy."

"It's a deal." Richard didn't care who won their competition. All he wanted was to spend time with his son. The last few years had changed both of them, and not in a good way. When depression and isolation had broken his spirit, Jack had helped him perform the most basic human rituals to get through each day. Between school and the chores he'd had to do, Jack's life hadn't been easy. And Richard regretted every moment he'd robbed his son of his childhood.

Jack flicked his right arm forward. The stone shot toward the water, hitting its icy coolness at a speed that sent it careening across the surface.

"Seven!" Jack shrieked. "It's a world record!"

Richard grinned and held up his stone. With the same technique Jack had used, he flung his stone toward the lake. It touched the first ripple, hit the water for a second time, and then sunk like a dead weight.

"Bad luck, Dad." The gleam in his son's eyes didn't bode well for the ice cream flavor he was choosing.

"Don't tell me we're eating pistachio and caramel again."

"You said the winner could have whatever they want."

With a mock sigh, Richard admitted defeat. "Fair enough. Let's walk for a little longer before we head into town. Where are you up to in the story you're writing?"

"The spaceship has just flown over Jupiter. Did you know Jupiter has four rings and they're made from teeny tiny pieces of dust?"

"I knew about the rings, but not what they're made from."

"Katie showed me a website with all kinds of cool stuff about the planets. When my spaceship flew through Jupiter's rings, everything jumped around and made a huge noise."

"Did it get damaged?"

Jack grinned. "If I told you, you'd guess what happens next."

"I'm curious. It's a great story." Richard stepped onto the boardwalk and winced.

"Is your leg sore?"

"A little." Being part of a trial for a new type of prosthetic limb had changed Richard's life, but that didn't stop the phantom pain shooting from his right thigh to where his toes would have been.

"Did you do your exercises?"

"I finished the second set before we left home." Richard placed his hand on Jack's shoulder. "I'll be okay."

"That's what you always say."

"Because it's true. Did Pastor John give you the new list of after-school programs?"

Jack nodded. "I need to choose what I want to do before the end of next week."

"Which ones do you like the best?"

"The gardening class with Mr. Jessop sounds like fun and there's a candy making class, too. I thought about joining the flower decorating class, but Charlie said that's for girls."

Richard's eyebrows rose. He didn't know what surprised him more; Jack's best friend's reaction or the image of Paris in her blue dress and red sneakers that filled his mind. "Everyone can enjoy flower decorating. Why do you want to do it?"

"I liked making a Christmas wreath last year. If I do the class, I could make something else for our house."

"That's a great idea."

"So, you think it's okay if I join the class?"

"I do. It sounds like fun."

Jack hurried toward some stones that were stacked on top of each other. They were all flat and perfect for skipping across the water. "Who do you think left them here?"

"Someone who thought another person would like skipping stones."

Reaching into his pocket, Jack placed two of his flattest stones onto the pile. "I don't need these ones anymore."

"Why are you leaving them here?"

"To make someone else happy."

The simple explanation humbled Richard. "That's a nice thing to do. How about we go to Sweet Treats now?"

Jack giggled as a gust of wind lifted his cap off his head. "Yes, please!"

Placing his stones on top of Jack's, Richard said a silent prayer of thanks. He didn't know what he'd done to deserve having him in his life, but he would always be grateful.

PARIS STOPPED her truck outside the cottages on Anchor Lane and turned off the engine. The last two days had been a whirlwind of activity. Kylie had considered her proposal and liked the idea of each business specializing in different types of clients. With that sorted, she'd met with Penny to see if the lease was still available on the first cottage.

Thankfully, no one else had asked about it. With a trembling hand, she'd signed a conditional lease subject to a start-up loan being approved by the bank.

Stepping out of her truck, she smiled at her two friends walking toward her. Kylie and Jackie were looking forward to seeing the cottage. "Don't be put off by what you see. After the construction crew has finished, it will be amazing."

Jackie hugged her. "I'm so excited. The cottage is in the perfect location. It's the first building people will see when they turn into Anchor Lane."

"I agree," Kylie said. "The outside of the building is full of character and charm. I can't wait to see what's inside."

Paris climbed the steps and unlocked the front door. "The contractors won't be back until Monday morning, so we can stay for as long as we like." Reaching into a box, she handed each of her friends a hard hat. "We need to wear these while we're looking around."

Kylie placed a hat on her head. "This reminds me of when I was remodeling Blooming Lovely."

"If the cottage looks as good as your flower shop, I'll be thrilled."

"All it takes is a little imagination and lots of patience," Kylie replied with a grin.

With her hat firmly in place, Jackie stepped into the room on the left-hand side of the entryway. "This is nice and sunny."

Paris pulled a folder out of her bag. "The afternoon sun streams through these windows. I thought this area would make a wonderful space for the sales counter and my work table. What do you think about these counter options?"

Jackie studied the pictures Paris had found in an online catalog. "They look lovely. Any of them would be perfect."

Kylie looked over Jackie's shoulder. "I agree, but my favorite is the bleached pine counter. The lighter color won't dominate the small space."

"I like that one, too." Paris crossed the hallway into the next room. "Come and have a look at the rest of the cottage. Richard's team has removed the wall between this room and the one at the back. This is where I'll showcase what I can do for large venues."

"With pictures of our previous jobs?" Jackie asked.

"Sort of. I thought I'd incorporate a large photo of an event, and then recreate an aspect of the photo in front of it. It could be a decorated arch, a table with a guest book and a flower arrangement, or a selection of wedding favors."

"You could make one of the gift baskets we gave the guests at the Mulligan's wedding. They were really cute."

Paris smiled. "That's a great idea."

Kylie walked to the back of the open-plan room. "You have enough floor space to be creative, but not too much that it becomes a burden. It will be fantastic when it's finished."

A weight lifted from Paris' shoulders. "I was worried you'd think I was trying to do too much."

Kylie's blue eyes sparkled. "If you don't try something new, nothing changes. Knowing you'll decorate the bigger events has taken a lot of stress out of my life. I'm looking forward to spending less time at Blooming Lovely and more time with my baby after she's born."

"And I'm looking forward to not working all hours of the day and night," Jackie added. "What are you looking forward to the most, Paris?"

She looked around the half-finished cottage and sighed. "I can't wait to own a business that makes a difference in people's lives. I couldn't have done it without you guys."

"That's what friends are for," Kylie murmured as she hugged Paris tight. "If you need any advice, come and see me."

Paris hoped she meant it, because the next twelve months could be full of surprises.

THE FOLLOWING WEEK, Richard carried a sheet of drywall into the first cottage on Anchor Lane. With the plumbers and electricians focusing on the kitchen and bathroom areas, the rest of the construction crew was making good progress. Next door, in the second cottage, bags of trash were being thrown in the dumpster, and some of the internal walls were being removed.

Overall, he was happy with their progress. He'd be even happier when his next delivery of supplies arrived. "Lean the drywall against here," he said to Tommy, one of the students in the Connect Church's construction program. "After we've brought the last sheet inside, we'll screw them to the walls."

Anyone would think he'd told him there was a check for a million dollars waiting outside. He moved twice as fast as they placed the sheets of drywall in front of some others.

If it weren't for Pastor John's apprenticeship program, Tommy and most of the teenagers Richard worked with would have left Sapphire Bay. Even with all the issues they'd had to overcome, taking on young people as apprentices was one of the most rewarding things he'd done.

"Excuse me," a familiar female voice said from the doorway. "Can I talk to you for a moment, Richard?"

He turned and had to look twice at Paris. Instead of the colorful clothes she usually wore, the black jeans and white T-shirt were oddly normal. "You aren't wearing your Dorothy of Oz dress."

"It's in my closet. I've finished work for the day."

"You're lucky. We still have another couple of hours ahead of us."

"That's why I'm here. Do you need a hand? I don't know much about construction, but I'm willing to learn."

Richard tried not to look surprised but, judging by Paris' reaction, he'd failed.

"Pastor John said you have a team of volunteers working on the cottages. I'm volunteering."

"Why? I thought you'd be busy at Blooming Lovely."

"When I saw what you're doing with the cottage, it inspired me. I thought about the types of businesses that could work from here and what they'd need."

Tommy bounced from one foot to the other. "While you're talking, I'll grab more drywall."

"Don't carry it inside on your own. Ask one of the other apprentices to help."

Paris moved out of Tommy's way as he hurried outside. "Did I interrupt what you're doing?"

"Don't worry. Tommy likes to be busy. Otherwise, he doesn't know what to do with himself."

"I used to be like that. Flower arranging helped me relax and focus on one thing at a time."

Richard picked up an electric drill. "If you know people who want to lease the cottages, you should speak to Penny. She's organizing the tenancy agreements."

"I've done that." Taking a sheet of paper out of her pocket, Paris dangled it in front of his nose. "Guess who's signed a conditional lease on this building?"

He looked into her eyes and frowned. She couldn't mean what he thought she did. Paris had a good job. Why would she give that up to lease one of the cottages? "I don't understand. You told me you enjoy working at Blooming Lovely."

Her eyes gleamed. "I do, but this was such an amazing opportunity. Kylie needs to work fewer hours and I want to own my own business. As long as the bank loans me some money, I'll be working full time from here."

"You'll be competing for the same customers."

"That's the great thing about what we've organized. Instead of doing the same thing, we're specializing in different types of clients. I'll provide the flower arrangements for large events and Blooming Lovely will provide the flowers for smaller gatherings. If an event is extra-large, we'll work on it together."

Richard checked the scaffolding they'd placed in front of a wall. "Owning a business isn't easy. Apart from making sure you have enough cash flow, you'll need a solid marketing plan to let people know you exist."

"Kylie has shown Jackie and me everything she does. I'm

organized and a hard worker. I'm not scared of working long hours if it means creating a better future for myself."

"All I'm saying is that owning a business is a big decision. Most small businesses don't make it past the first year."

"Why do you always have to be so negative?"

"I'm being realistic." Richard glanced over Paris' shoulder. Tommy and another apprentice were carrying a few sheets of drywall into the room. "If you think you can start a new business, go for it."

Her mouth clamped together in a straight line. "I shouldn't have said anything." She stepped out of Tommy's way. "Good luck with the cottage. I'll let you know what happens."

Before Richard could reply, Paris left the room.

His hand tightened around the drill. Sometimes, he wished he didn't say the first thing that hit his brain. He didn't mean to be negative but, from what he'd seen, Paris had a way of glossing over the bad things in life. He knew how hard it was to run a successful business, but he wasn't sure she did.

"Where would you like the drywall, boss?" Tommy asked.

"Leave it against the far wall." With the completion date of the cottage looming, he couldn't afford to be distracted by a woman wearing black jeans and a white T-shirt. But, as he helped Tommy lift a sheet of drywall into place, he felt like an idiot. Paris had arrived at the cottage full of enthusiasm and excitement. She'd left looking miserable.

He just hoped she knew what she was doing.

CHAPTER 4

*P*astor John walked into the room Paris was using for the junior floral decorating class. "You're early," he said. "I didn't think you'd be here until three-thirty."

"Jackie offered to close Blooming Lovely, so I thought I'd come here to work on my business case for the cottage." She'd told John about starting her own business. At least he'd been enthusiastic, unlike someone else she knew.

"How's it going?"

"Slow. I need to provide a spreadsheet showing projected sales and expenses for the next twelve months. Kylie gave me a copy of her income and expenditure sheet, so I'm using that as a guide."

"When does it need to be finished?"

"Next week." Paris forced a smile. "How's your day?"

"It's been eventful. We received funding for the redevelopment of the community garden."

"That's fantastic." Pastor John had applied to all kinds of funders to expand their community vegetable garden. "Does that mean we'll see more greenhouses in the backyard?"

"That's the plan. The company that supplied the last one has a backlog of orders, so it could take a few months. I know someone who can help you with the documentation for the bank."

"Everyone at the church is already busy. I'll be okay."

"I'm sure you will, but it's no bother. Shelley has helped a few people with new business loans."

She should turn down Pastor John's offer, but his wife was an accountant. If anyone could save her hours of work, it was Shelley. "Are you sure she has the time to help me?"

"If she doesn't, she'll tell us." John checked his watch. "We could ask her now if you like?"

Paris' eyes skimmed across the flowers, wire, and foliage on each table. Everything was ready for the class. "That sounds like a great idea. Is she in her office?"

"She was there ten minutes ago. If she's gone, Andrea will know where she is."

After she'd slipped her laptop into its case, Paris added the notes she'd made for her application. She'd never asked for so much money in her life but, if she didn't have enough working capital, her business would fail before it began.

"What are you calling your flower shop?" Pastor John asked as they walked out of the room.

"The Flower Cottage." His thoughtful expression worried Paris. "Is it too plain?"

"It doesn't need to be fancy. I like it. Once your customers visit the cottage, they'll never forget your name."

"I hope so. Kylie said it's important to have the right branding. Otherwise, there's a disconnect between what people expect to see and what they actually get."

"In that case, The Flower Cottage is perfect." As they walked along the corridor, Jack Dawkins hurried toward them. "Hi, Pastor John. My friend's mom dropped me off early. Can I wait in the dining room?"

"We can do better than that. Mrs. Terry just took some chewy chocolate chip cookies out of the oven. If you go into the kitchen, she might let you have one."

"Okay. Hi, Paris. I'm coming to your workshop. Dad thought it was a great idea."

Paris' eyes widened. "He did?"

"I told him how much I liked making the Christmas wreaths. Are we making them again?"

"We are, but not today. We're making some special Valentine's Day flowers this afternoon."

"I could give mine to Dad." With an excited grin, Jack looked at Pastor John. "But don't tell him. It's a surprise."

"Your secret's safe with me." John rested his hand on Jack's shoulder and nudged him toward the kitchen. "Tell Mrs. Terry to save some cookies for Paris and me."

"I will." With a quick wave, he ran toward the kitchen.

Pastor John smiled. "If the rest of the class is as excited as Jack, they won't want the program to end."

"We had the same problem in December. I think that's why Kylie asked me to run these sessions. She didn't like turning people away because the class was full."

"We could always run another program after this one's finished?"

Paris laughed. John was always trying to find tutors for the church's programs. "Nice try, but I'm already doing five sessions with the children, and the next adult class is full. Ask me again after The Flower Cottage opens."

"I'll do that." John tapped on an open office door and smiled at his wife. "Is it okay if we interrupt?"

Shelley smiled. "Of course, it is. Hi, Paris. John's not twisting your arm about tutoring more classes, is he?"

"Only a little. I'm hoping you'll help me complete a business loan application. But, if you don't have enough time, I understand."

"I'm happy to help. How far along are you?"

"About halfway. I have to run a class in about twenty minutes, but I could come back another day."

"Now that you're here, why don't you show me what you've done? After that, we'll work out how much extra time it will take."

John pulled a chair closer to Shelley's desk. "While you're talking, I'll follow Jack into the kitchen. Mabel might need a hand with the cookies."

"Don't eat them all," Shelley told him.

"I wouldn't dream of it. I'll see you both later."

Paris sat opposite Shelley. It would take more than a few minutes to show her what she'd done—and even longer to fill out the rest of the information. She just hoped Shelley didn't think she was crazy to want to start her own business.

Opening her folder, she handed Shelley the application form and Kylie's spreadsheet. "I feel like I'm sinking in quicksand. I understand most of the questions, but I don't know how to estimate my income."

"Everyone has the same problem. Don't worry. We'll work it out together." After spending the next ten minutes reading what Paris had brought with her, Shelley sat back and smiled. "You're farther ahead than you think. Why don't I send you a list of additional information we'll need? Once I have that, we should be able to complete the forms in about two hours. Does that work for you?"

Paris sighed. "It sounds perfect."

Shelley laughed. "That's one of the most enthusiastic responses I've had today."

"It's probably because I'm desperate."

Sitting closer to her keyboard, Shelley started typing. "Once you know what you're doing, you won't be desperate anymore."

She hoped Shelley was right. Regardless of how confident

Paris felt, owning a business was a huge commitment. Especially to someone who'd never committed to anything in their life.

"YOU SHOULD HAVE SEEN what Nora made, Dad. Her sunflower bouquet was amazing."

From the moment Richard had collected Jack from The Welcome Center, he'd talked non-stop about what had happened in the flower decorating class. "What did you make?"

Jack grinned. "It's a surprise."

"Let me know if you want me to help you bring it home."

"It's okay. Paris said she'd help me."

That sounded like something she'd say. He had no idea what Jack's flower arrangement would look like, but he did have some exciting news. "I met a lady today who's donating enough money to build three tiny homes."

Jack waved at Mr. Penman, one of the oldest residents in the tiny home village. "Will she be our neighbor?"

"No. She doesn't live in Sapphire Bay anymore. She's visiting her friends. The thing is, she still owns a house on the edge of town, and she doesn't need it anymore. She asked Pastor John if he knew anyone who'd want to buy it."

"Stacey and her mom are moving into a new house tomorrow. Stacey's painting her bedroom pink and purple, 'cos they're her favorite colors."

"She must be looking forward to that." He studied Jack's face. "What if we moved into a new house?"

"Like Stacey?"

Richard nodded.

"What about our friends? I'll miss them."

"We'd still be living close to the village. We could invite

our friends to our new house." The earnest expression on Jack's face tore at Richard's heart. With everything his son had been through, any change to his routine was difficult. "We wouldn't be moving straightaway. I'll need to talk to the bank to see if they'll lend me some money."

Bending down, Jack took the front door key out of a box they'd hidden under a rock. "Paris visited the bank. She wants to open a flower shop."

"I know. I'm remodeling the cottage she'd like to use."

Jack's eyes widened. "You are?"

"If she gets the loan, she'll be able to decorate the store exactly how she wants."

"I hope she can open her store. She said no one in her family has ever owned a business." Lifting his backpack off his shoulders, Jack climbed the stairs into the loft.

Richard wondered what else Paris had told the group of eager flower enthusiasts. "Would you like a glass of milk before dinner?"

"No, thanks." Jack's head appeared over the rail. "If we move, can I have a puppy or a kitten?"

From the first day they'd arrived in Sapphire Bay, Jack had wanted a pet. Mr. Snuggles, The Welcome Center's resident rescue cat, had filled the void in his son's life. But, if they moved farther away, he wouldn't see him as often.

The worried frown on Jack's face made Richard's decision for him. "A kitten would be okay. We could visit the animal shelter and see if they have any that need a home."

"Yeah!"

"I'll have to talk to Pastor John first. Someone else might buy the house."

"I know." Jack climbed down the stairs. "If we move into the lady's house, will it be our forever home?"

"I hope so." He knew how important having somewhere to call home was to Jack. "I had a look at the house this morning. It has a swing hanging from a big apple tree in the backyard. We could build a treehouse and make the property ours."

With a contented sigh, Jack sat at their small dining table and pulled out his homework. "It sounds like a nice house. Grandma could visit us."

Richard took some chicken out of the refrigerator and thought about his mom. "She would enjoy that. What homework do you have?"

"I need to finish a story and do a worksheet for math."

"Let me know if you need help."

"Okay." Jack bent his head and started writing.

If living in their own home was a big deal for Jack, it was even bigger for Richard. It would give him a sense of permanence, a safety net he hadn't had in years. But, mostly, it symbolized a new beginning, the start of something that would provide a brighter future for him and his son.

PARIS TAPPED her pen against her chin. After speaking with Shelley, completing the bank's application form wasn't quite so daunting. They'd increased the expenses Paris expected to have and reduced her projected sales. Her net profit wasn't as generous, but it gave her more wiggle room if something unexpected happened.

The one thing she hadn't factored into her budget was the cost of advertising. Hopefully, some of the low-cost ideas Shelley gave her would be enough to attract new clients to The Flower Cottage.

A knock on her front door was a welcome distraction. Leaving everything on the table, she walked into the entryway.

As soon as she opened the door, her friend Andrea

hurried inside. "Thank goodness you're here. I only have a few minutes before I have to pick up the boys from school."

"What's happened?"

"Nothing. In fact, everything couldn't be better." Reaching into her bag, she pulled out her cell phone. "I saw some shelving on eBay that I thought would be perfect for your store."

Paris had to look twice to make sure the wrought iron shelving with white-painted shelves wasn't the same furniture she'd found at an online store. "It's similar to the furniture I was going to order."

"I thought so. Look at the price."

She couldn't believe it. "That's half what the other supplier was charging."

"I forgot what you told me, but these shelves sounded a lot cheaper. And the quality is really good. Take a look at the reviews."

By the time Paris had finished reading the reviews, she knew it was worth buying one set to see if they were okay. "Can you send me a link to the page? If I place an order today, it should arrive next week."

Andrea's eyes widened. "Has the bank approved your loan?"

Paris sighed. "Not yet. I'm still filling out the forms."

"Don't worry. Everyone wants to see new businesses opening in Sapphire Bay."

"I hope they take that into consideration."

"I'm sure they will. But the shelving wasn't the only reason I stopped by. I wanted to tell you how much Charlie enjoyed your flower arranging class."

"I thought he did. I was surprised by how many great ideas everyone had for their Valentine's Day gifts."

"That's because you're such an amazing teacher. Charlie said Jack was in the class, too."

Paris handed Andrea her phone. "I don't like the gleam in your eyes."

"You forgot to mention that Jack's dad is remodeling the cottage you want to lease."

"It didn't seem important."

Andrea grinned. "He's the only person who's ruffled your feathers since you moved here. Have you ever thought there might be a reason for that?"

"I know the reason, and it isn't what you think. Richard has a habit of thinking the worst of a situation. It's so annoying."

"And you think everything will be perfect. Maybe that annoys him."

"I don't know why it would." Paris looked a little closer at her friend. "How did you know Richard's remodeling the cottages?"

"I walked down Anchor Lane yesterday to see what was happening. He was there with Penny."

"The cottages will look incredible when they're finished."

Andrea touched her arm. "And one of them will be yours. The loans officer won't turn down your application."

"I hope not. Thanks for showing me the shelving."

"You're welcome. If you see Richard, be kind to him. He's been through a lot in the last few years."

Paris frowned. "What do you know that I don't?"

"You'll have to ask him. Are you coming to the Valentine's Day party at The Welcome Center?"

"I'm not sure. It's one of Blooming Lovely's busiest days."

"It won't matter if you're late." Andrea checked her watch. "I have to go. Let me know when the shelving arrives and I'll help you put it together."

"Thanks. That would be great."

As soon as Andrea was gone, Paris returned to the kitchen and picked up her pen. Shelley had offered to go over everything once she'd answered the questions. Hopefully, when the loans officer saw her application, she wouldn't say no. If she did, Paris would be disappointed, but there was always a silver lining to everything that happened. Sometimes, you just had to search a little deeper to find it.

CHAPTER 5

*R*ichard glanced at the paper hearts and red balloons strung around the large meeting room. Coming to The Welcome Center for a party celebrating love and romance wasn't high on his list of priorities. But, Jack had insisted, and he couldn't say no.

"Do you like the flowers?" Jack asked excitedly.

Each table held a vase filled with red and white daisies. "They're great. Is that what you were doing this afternoon?" Jack and some of his friends had met Paris here after school. Their top-secret mission was to decorate the room without anyone, apart from Pastor John, seeing it.

"We made the flower arrangements and put the chairs around the tables. Pastor John had already blown up the balloons and hung them everywhere."

"You did a good job."

"There's Charlie and Andy." Jack pointed to two of his friends. "Can I talk to them?"

"Of course, you can. I'll be waiting over here."

As soon as Jack left, Andrea Smith, Charlie and Andy's mom, stood beside him holding two glasses of juice. "I thought you might like this." She handed Richard one of the drinks. "Jack didn't know if you'd be here, but it's great you could make it."

"I didn't have a choice," he said with a smile. "Jack reminded me at least a dozen times about the party."

"They've been planning it for the last couple of weeks. The hospitality class made the food, and Mabel Terry donated the juice and decorations."

Richard looked across the room. There was enough food to feed half of Sapphire Bay. "Everyone's been busy."

Andrea nodded. "I saw Paris yesterday. She's excited about opening a flower shop."

"I hope the bank approves her loan."

"So do I. You know, you have a lot in common."

He frowned. Paris had just walked into the party wearing a white dress with red hearts sewn around the hem. A red cape with glittery edges sparkled as she waved to someone she knew. Richard couldn't think of anyone he had less in common with.

"We're the complete opposite."

Andrea shrugged. "Maybe on the outside, but you both came here to start over. You're stubborn, determined, and put other people before yourselves. And, if that isn't enough similarities, you've also started your own businesses. Just think of all the advice you could give her."

"I'm not looking for anyone special in my life. If you think Paris and I—"

"I wasn't trying to play Cupid."

"That's good because I'm happy on my own."

Paris chose that moment to look across the room. When her eyes connected with his, a jolt of electricity shot through him. That wasn't anything unusual where she was concerned. Paris got under his skin and taunted him with her quirky sense of humor and ridiculous positivity. He was attracted to her, but he wouldn't do anything about it.

He was old enough to realize that physical attraction wasn't what kept people together. What kept them together were all the things he'd never be able to give anyone.

"Don't look so worried," Andrea whispered.

That was easy for her to say. Jack had hurried across to Paris and was grinning like he'd discovered a pot of gold. It didn't matter to his son that she was wearing an over-the-top costume or that nearly every person in the room was looking at her.

To his dismay, Jack pointed to him, then said something to Paris. Her smile disappeared and she shook her head.

Even from across the room, he knew she didn't want to talk to him.

Jack wasn't deterred. With a little more coaxing, they slowly made their way toward him.

"I knew she'd come and say hello," Andrea said with more enthusiasm than he felt. "Maybe she's heard from the bank."

It probably had more to do with Jack. But, instead of continuing toward them, they walked into the kitchen. A few seconds later, Jack appeared holding a box.

Richard glanced at Andrea. "Do you know what Jack's holding?"

Her smile told him she knew exactly what it was. "Charlie gave me a similar box before we came here. Apart from that, I'm not saying anything."

By the time Jack was beside him, he was almost certain it was the flower arrangement his son had made in Paris' class.

"Happy Valentine's Day, Dad," Jack said proudly. "This is for you."

Richard glanced at the wary look in Paris' eyes before holding the box. "Thank you. Should I open it here or at home?"

"Here."

Kneeling, he peeled off the tape. When he saw the wire-framed motorcycle with tiny flowers woven through the wheels, he smiled.

Jack moved closer. "When we were in Los Angeles, Grandma showed me lots of photos of you riding a motorcycle. Before we made the Valentine's Day presents, Paris said to think of something that was special for our parents. I thought you must like motorcycles because you rode them so much."

Richard took his gift out of the box. Until he'd joined the army, his life had revolved around when he could ride with his friends. They'd traveled from one side of the country to the other, seeing places they didn't know existed and meeting people who were just as crazy as them.

"Do you like it?"

"I love it." He wrapped his arm around Jack and kissed the side of his head. "It's the best Valentine's Day present I've ever been given."

"Paris helped me make it. We found a photo of a motorcycle on the Internet and copied its shape."

Carefully, he placed it on the table and looked up at Paris. "Thank you."

"You're welcome," she said softly.

Andrea looked across the room. "John's ready to welcome everyone. Do you want me to put your gift in the small meeting room with the others? It will be safer there."

"I can drop it off," Richard told her.

"I have to go there, anyway. Why don't you stay with Paris? She can tell you what's happening with the bank."

Paris frowned. "There isn't a lot to say. I've submitted my loan application. All I can do is wait for their decision."

"At least you're through the first hurdle," Andrea said. "I'll be back soon."

After an awkward moment of silence, Richard cleared his throat. "I like your costume."

Paris ran her hands along the skirt of the dress. "It's the Queen of Hearts, from *Alice in Wonderland*. Jackie helped me make it." She looked uncertainly at him. "I'm sorry about the other day. I shouldn't have stomped out of the cottage."

"I'm sorry, too. You were excited about opening a flower shop and I made you feel bad."

Jack looked at his dad. "What did you say?"

"I told Paris owning a business is hard."

"That's what you told me about playing basketball." Jack turned to Paris. "All my friends are tall and I couldn't shoot hoops when they stood over me. Dad showed me a super-cool move that helps." Jack bounced an imaginary ball, stepped to the left, and then pivoted to the right as he threw his shot into the air. "They don't know where I'm going."

Paris smiled. "I'll have to remember that next time someone stands in my way."

Richard's shoulders relaxed as he watched the easy friendship between Paris and his son. "Do you play basketball?" he asked her.

"No, but I enjoy watching it. I've been to a few games at the church, but I haven't seen you and Jack there."

"We go sometimes," Jack said. "Especially since Dad got his new leg. It makes it easier for him to walk."

Paris nodded. "I read about his prosthetic leg in the newspaper. It sounds amazing."

"It's changed my life." Richard couldn't begin to describe how much it had helped.

"Dad doesn't need to use his wheelchair anymore."

Paris' eyes lifted to Richard's. "I didn't realize you couldn't walk."

"I walked, but it was painful." The sympathy in her eyes made him feel uncomfortable. "I don't need your pity."

43

Paris didn't take offence at his softly spoken words. "Don't worry. I wasn't going to give you any."

He breathed a sigh of relief when Pastor John tapped the top of the microphone. At least for now, he wouldn't have to answer the questions Paris was bound to have.

"Welcome to our Valentine's Day party," John said from the front of the room.

As he thanked the people who'd made today possible, Richard glanced at Paris. She looked oddly endearing in her Queen of Hearts costume.

He had no idea why she liked dressing up or why she wanted to own a flower shop. Maybe, if he told her about his life, she'd tell him about hers. But that meant sharing a part of himself that made him feel raw and vulnerable, and he didn't know if he could do it.

PARIS STOOD in front of the general store, staring at her cell phone. Two minutes and fifteen seconds ago, the loans officer at the bank had sent her an email.

"Are you okay?"

Lifting her gaze, Paris looked into the worried face of her friend, Andrea. "The bank sent me an email."

"About your loan application?"

"I haven't opened it, but I think so."

"That was quick." Andrea pulled her across to a wooden seat. "Are they lending you the money?"

"I don't know. I haven't opened the message."

Andrea frowned. "What are you worried about?"

There were so many things that she didn't know where to start. "If they say no, I won't be able to open my own business."

"From what you said, Shelley seemed positive about your application."

"She was, but she isn't the person making the decision."

Andrea's steady gaze made Paris' heart sink. The reason she hadn't opened the email went a lot deeper than worrying about the bank's decision, and her friend knew it.

"Is this about what your mother said?"

"I shouldn't listen to her, but she's my mom." Paris' relationship with her family was complicated. Her mom was a high-functioning alcoholic who bounced from one bad relationship to the next. For most of her childhood, Paris had lived with her grandma, trying to ignore the chaos around her.

It didn't matter how hard she tried to make her mom happy; it never worked. "What if she's right? I don't know anything about owning a successful business. If I fail, it could ruin my credit rating and make it difficult to do other things."

"You have more support here than you ever did back home. Shelley's an accountant. She would have told you if it wasn't the right thing to do."

Paris looked at her phone.

"Measuring yourself by your mom's standards is a waste of time. She abandoned you more times than you can remember. If nothing in your life ever changed from today, you'd still be a better person than she'll ever be."

"She tried her best."

"Did she?"

Andrea's gentle question unsettled Paris more than she wanted to admit. As an adult, she knew her mom could have done more. But, as a child, she'd always thought the best of her. Always thought her mom wanted the best for both of them.

"You're a great florist. Open the email. At least then you won't be wondering what the loans officer said."

With a trembling hand, Paris tapped on the message. She skimmed through the text, breathing a sigh of relief when she saw the bank's decision. "I've got it. The bank will lend me the money."

Andrea grinned. "That's fantastic. Congratulations."

Paris hugged her friend. "Thank you. I would have spent most of the day worrying about the email."

"That's what friends are for. What's next?"

"I have to make an appointment to sign the loan documents. After that, I need to work out what I want to do inside the cottage." Taking a deep breath, she read the email again. "I can't believe I'll finally own my own flower shop."

"Your grandma would have been proud of you."

Paris nodded. It was a shame her mother would never feel the same way.

CHAPTER 6

*R*ichard stopped in front of the first cottage on Anchor Lane. He'd spent most of the day at the old steamboat museum, creating furniture for his own business. Between that and overseeing the construction crews working on the tiny homes and the cottages, there were never enough hours in the day.

Thankfully, everything was running to schedule. By the end of next week, three more tiny homes would be driven to Wyoming for a social housing development. By the end of March, twenty families would be living in safe and warm houses designed for people who have experienced chronic homelessness.

If that wasn't enough good news, orders for his outdoor furniture were growing. More than one client had been so impressed they'd returned for additional pieces. Hopefully, if sales continued to increase, he could resign from his job on the tiny home project and focus on his own work.

"Hey, boss. Did you pick up the extra platforms for the ladders?"

Richard opened his door and moved to the back of the

truck. "They're in here. I threw in a couple of charger's for the power drills, too. It looked as though someone forgot theirs yesterday."

Tommy sent him a lopsided grin. "I didn't think you'd notice."

"Hard not to when you disappeared so often."

"I had to wait until someone finished charging their batteries before doing mine. It worked out okay."

"It will work out better with these." Richard picked up the rechargers and a bucket of primer. "Has Paris told anyone what colored paint she wants?"

"Not yet, but you can ask her yourself." Tommy looked over Richard's shoulder. "What's she wearing?"

Richard turned and sighed. Today's outfit was a vibrant mix of red, yellow, and orange flowers. It didn't surprise him that she'd chosen a dress that looked like a bouquet of flowers.

Tommy was still staring at Paris, not that Richard could blame him. "You'd better take the platform inside before the boss gets grumpy."

With a heartfelt sigh, Tommy slid a platform out of the truck. But, instead of taking it inside, he waited for Paris to join them. "Nice dress, ma'am."

She sent him a dimple-laden grin. "Thanks. Did Richard tell you I'm leasing the first cottage?"

"He did. You must be excited."

"I am. I just met with a couple who are getting married in April. If they let me create the flowers for their wedding, they'll be one of The Flower Cottage's first clients."

"That's awesome."

Richard cleared his throat.

"I gotta go," Tommy said. "Let me know if you need help with anything."

"That's so sweet. Thank you."

48

Richard lifted two buckets of undercoat out of the truck. "I have the list of ideas you sent me."

"What did you think?"

"The layout makes sense, although I'm not sure about the shelves. They may not be sturdy enough."

"The set I ordered should be here tomorrow. Can I show you them to see what you think?"

"Of course, you can. I'll look through the catalogs in my office, too. There might be something else that's better. Have you decided what color you're painting the walls?"

Paris showed him the bags she was carrying. "I painted a set of canvas blocks with some options. It will be easier to choose a color after I see them in the rooms."

Richard nodded toward the cottage. "I'll follow you." With a pair of impossibly high heels clicking against the pavement, Paris sashayed up the garden path. "Remember to wear a hard hat and sign the site register."

"How could I forget," she said sweetly.

Another apprentice walked out of the house and stopped when he saw Paris. "Hi. It's good to see you again."

"It's nice to see you, too, Dave. Thanks for the advice. Mabel and Allan had plenty of paint samples to choose from." She left the bags on the porch and pulled out a canvas block. "This is one of the colors I like. What do you think?"

"It's a great shade of white."

Paris smiled. The kind of smile that could turn a man's head. "It's called natural beige."

Dave's eyebrows rose. "It looks white."

Richard cleared his throat. Dave was here to work, not socialize with an attractive brunette in a crazy dress. "Did you need something, Dave?"

"I'm meeting Pastor John at the old steamboat museum. Is there anything you need?"

"Not at the moment."

"In that case, I'll see you tomorrow." He sent Paris a cheeky grin. "I'm glad you found some paint you like."

"You were a great help," Paris said. "Thank you."

"You're welcome." With his knight in shining armor moment complete, Dave left the cottage.

Richard picked up the paint buckets. If his construction crew took as much interest in the job as they did in Paris, they'd finish a lot sooner. Hopefully, Paris would be too busy organizing her new business to visit them again. But, remembering the excited look she'd sent Tommy and Dave, it was extremely unlikely.

"ARE YOU SURE?" Richard studied the canvas block leaning against the drywall. "Won't navy blue be too dark?" If Paris wanted blue, he preferred the lighter shade beside it.

"This area gets a lot of natural light, so it can take a slightly darker color. And the blue walls will look gorgeous behind the wooden shelving I've chosen."

"What about the other rooms?"

"I'd like something more sophisticated for the display room, kitchen, and bathroom." She walked into the next room and placed three canvases against the wall. With her head tilted sideways, she studied each color. "I still like natural beige. It's the one in the middle."

"I can see why Dave thought it was white."

Paris nibbled her bottom lip. "Do you think it's too pale? It's supposed to be slightly darker than cream but not too brown."

"I'm the worst person to ask for color advice. If you like it, use it. You can always paint the walls a different color later on."

"That's true." With a decisive nod, Paris picked up the

canvases. "I'll have natural beige in this room, the kitchen, and the bathroom, and navy blue in the sales area."

Richard typed the colors into the project plan. "Ceilings and trim?"

"Alabaster."

"White it is," he muttered. "I'll buy the paint in the morning. We should have the first coat finished by tomorrow evening."

"That's fast."

"It isn't a big space. How was work?"

"Busy. We're providing the flowers for three events this weekend. We've finished some of the arrangements, but not all of them. I'm going back to Blooming Lovely after I've seen you."

He checked his watch. "It's five o'clock. Shouldn't you be going home and doing whatever you do to relax?"

"Flower arranging relaxes me, especially if it's for an event I'm looking forward to. That's probably why I don't have much of a social life."

"You don't need a social life when you enjoy what you do."

"What do you like doing when you aren't working?"

Richard frowned. Between looking after his son, working part-time at the old steamboat museum, and running his own business, he didn't have much free time. "I spend time with Jack. We walk or ride around Flathead Lake. Sometimes we go to Polson or Bigfork."

"The weekend market in Bigfork is amazing. I've bought some lovely gifts from there." Paris poked her head around the kitchen doorframe. "You did a lot today."

"You can thank the construction crew for that. They're on track with all the alterations."

Tommy walked into the room. "See you later, boss. I've

left my batteries in the kitchen on the charger. They'll be ready for tomorrow."

"I'll lock the cottage before I leave. See you tomorrow."

With Tommy and the other apprentices gone for the day, Richard looked around the room. "We'll install the air conditioning after the walls are painted. You won't get cold over the winter with the extra insulation we've added."

"I appreciate everything you're doing. Penny must have invested a lot of money into the remodeling. Is there anything else you need from me before I leave?"

Richard looked through the project plan. "The paint colors were the most urgent. I'll let you know about the shelving."

"Thanks." Paris picked up the canvas blocks.

Richard cleared his throat. "I wanted to thank you for the motorcycle you helped Jack make. The flowers lasted longer than I thought they would."

"It was a great Valentine's Day present."

"I was surprised Jack wanted to join the flower decorating class. But, now that I've seen what you're doing, it's easy to see why he enjoys it."

Paris smiled. "You aren't the only parent who was confused. Andrea's boys were so excited she thought the name of the class was a secret code for online gaming."

"That would be Jack's idea of heaven, too." He handed Paris another canvas. "Why did you become a florist?"

Paris' smile dimmed, then resurfaced almost too brightly. "It wasn't something I'd thought about until I moved here. Kylie ran some flower decorating classes at the church and then offered me a part-time job. The more I learned, the more I loved it. I can't imagine doing anything else now."

"What did you do before you moved to Sapphire Bay?"

"I've tried a lot of jobs. I was a data analyst for a few years, a receptionist at an art gallery, a janitor, and a telemarketer.

Sales weren't my thing. I spent too much time listening to people tell me about their lives instead of selling them products."

"The people you called must have enjoyed the conversation."

Paris frowned. "They did, but I didn't earn enough commission to pay my rent. I have a problem with stick-ability."

"Stickability?"

"Most of the jobs I've had have only lasted for a year or two."

"You're still a florist."

Paris' hands tightened around the canvases. "I guess I've changed."

Richard wondered what he'd said to make her frown. "Would you like a ride to Blooming Lovely? I could drop you off on my way to The Welcome Center."

"I'll be okay. It's only a five-minute walk."

"Are you sure?"

"Positive. Thanks for looking at my ideas."

Richard nodded. "That's what I'm here to do."

"Enjoy the rest of the evening. If you have any questions, I'll be at Blooming Lovely until about nine o'clock."

Holding open the door, he watched her leave. So much for trying to understand Paris. All he'd done was make her look uncomfortable. Again.

"YOU'RE AWFULLY QUIET," Jackie said as she added another rose to a bouquet. "Did something happen at the cottage?"

Paris glanced at her friend before reaching for another flower. "Everything's fine. Richard said the first coat of paint should be on the walls by tomorrow night."

"That's fantastic. But, if the remodeling is going to plan, why do you look so worried?"

"I can't stop thinking that I've forgotten something."

"Have you checked the project plan you worked on with Shelley and Kylie?"

"I've looked at it so many times it's embedded in my brain."

Jackie handed her a blue ribbon. "Is there anything you still need to do?"

"No. Everything has been ticked off or is in the process of being finished. The only thing I'm worried about is the shelves. Richard thought the set I've ordered won't be strong enough to take the weight of the flowers."

"Did he have any suggestions on how you could make them sturdier?"

"He said he'd have a look at the sample set when it arrives. There might be a bracket or something he can add." Paris tied a ribbon around the bouquet she was making and held it toward Jackie. "What do you think?"

"It's perfect." With a flourish, she ticked a box on the spreadsheet behind them. "Four down, one to go. It's not often we have to make five bridesmaids' bouquets for a wedding."

"I don't have enough friends to invite five people to walk down the aisle with me."

Jackie laughed. "Same here. If we ever get married, promise me you'll be my bridesmaid. Otherwise, I'll be walking down the aisle on my own."

The weight on Paris' shoulders lifted. "I promise to be your bridesmaid as long as you'll be mine."

"It's a deal," Jackie said with a grin. "You do realize there's a significant issue with our forward planning, don't you?

Paris carried the bouquet across to the large refrigerator. "Would that be our terrible dating history, the lack of single men in Sapphire Bay, or not having enough time to talk to anyone outside of work?"

"When you put it like that, I think we should prepare for a long single life."

After Paris' disastrous dating experience, the thought of being single was more appealing than having her heart broken again. "Just think of all the extra money we'll have. We can travel the world, stay in exclusive resorts, and drink as many frozen margaritas as we like."

"You could open a chain of flower cottages around the world. I'll help you find the best locations and train other florists."

"We'll take the world by storm," Paris said as she picked up a stem of foliage. "One store at a time."

"What are we?"

Paris smiled as she remembered the positive mantra they'd repeated when they started working with Kylie. "We're positive, gorgeous, intelligent women who only need chocolate to be happy."

Reaching into her bag, Jackie pulled out two Snickers bars. "Amen to that."

And, with a smile that was just as content as Jackie's, Paris tore off one of the wrappers and bit into the soft, gooey center. Except for when she was dreaming about her new business, life didn't get much better than this.

CHAPTER 7

*R*ichard took a metal bracket out of his toolbox. The shelving unit Paris had ordered arrived this afternoon. Instead of leaving it until tomorrow to assemble, he'd stopped by her house after work.

Paris leaned over his shoulder, watching what he was doing as if it was complicated heart surgery. "Do you think it will make a difference?"

"It will be better than what was there. The shelves were only designed for office storage." He felt her curious blue eyes settle on his face. It had been a long time since a woman had stood so close to him. He'd forgotten the intimacy a softly spoken word could create. The awareness a woman like Paris could generate.

"Where did you learn to fix things?"

He tightened the screw and started on the next one. "My dad taught me. When I was little, I followed him around the house, watching what he did. He gave me my first tool belt when I was four."

"That must have been fun. You'd never have to throw anything away."

Richard's lips twitched. "Mom wasn't always happy. Dad wanted to fix things instead of buying new ones. They're still using the same toaster they were given when they got married." He attached the last screw and tried wiggling the shelf. "That's better."

Paris picked up a flower pot that was sitting on the veranda. "This is about the weight of the heaviest arrangement that will be on the shelves. I hope it works." With the pot sitting on the shelf, she slowly moved her hands away. With a grin that made him feel weirdly proud, she said, "It works!"

He gave the shelf another nudge, just to make sure. Nothing moved. "Not bad for a set of three-dollar brackets. Are you happy with how it looks?"

She looked closely at the shelving unit. "It's fine. You can hardly notice the brackets against the rest of the frame. I'll order the other shelving units tonight."

"How many do you need?"

"About five."

Richard screwed another bracket into the next shelf. "Let me know when they arrive. I'll put the brackets on for you."

"It's okay. I can do it."

His eyebrows rose. "You'll need a screwdriver."

"Stay here." Paris ran inside. When she came back, she was carrying a shiny, new screwdriver set. "Andrea gave me this as a housewarming present. It's the best thing anyone has ever given me."

Richard frowned. Either Paris set her sights low, or no one appreciated her for who she was. "That's the first time anyone's told me tools are better than flowers."

"I'm surrounded by flowers at work. I prefer practical, no-nonsense gifts that last forever. Let me do the next bracket."

"It will be easier with an electric drill."

She tapped his chest with one of the screwdrivers. "Are you scared I'll do a better job than you?"

"It's impossible to improve on perfection."

"Really?" Paris took a bracket out of the packet and sent him a superior smile. "As well as being incredibly practical, I'm a fast learner."

"That won't work."

"Why?"

"You have the wrong screwdriver. You need a flat head."

"A what?"

Reaching into the box, he pulled out a different screwdriver. "This one." Her smile told him she wasn't intimidated by his superior knowledge.

"I was testing you." And with an efficiency that surprised him, she attached the bracket. "Easy."

"I'm impressed." Reluctantly, he checked his watch. "As much as I've enjoyed helping you, I need to leave. Jack's after-school program is nearly finished, and I have more work to do."

Paris seemed almost as disappointed as he was that he had to leave.

"Before you go, I've got something for you." She left the screwdriver with the others and disappeared inside.

By the time he'd closed his toolbox, Paris was back holding a container. "Jack said you like chocolate muffins."

"You didn't need to bake me anything."

"Yes, I did. I appreciate you helping me with the shelves. I know how busy you are."

Richard lifted a corner of the lid. The sweet, rich scent of chocolate wafted through the air.

"I used my gran's recipe. I hope you like them."

"I'm sure I will. Thanks." He looked at Paris. Now would be a good time to tell her why he was cautious when she spoke about her new business. "There's a reason

I don't get excited when you talk about The Flower Cottage."

"It doesn't matter."

"Yes, it does. I know what it's like to start a business. Last year, I made some furniture for a friend. After a lot of hard work, I opened a part-time business making furniture for other people. It's easy to underestimate how much time and energy it will take." He handed her a business card and watched her expression change from confusion to surprise.

"I've seen your furniture. Kylie and Ben said a local craftsperson made their dining room table. It's beautiful."

"It was one of the first pieces I sold. I'm focusing on outdoor furniture, but I create commission pieces if my clients want them."

Paris frowned. "Why didn't you tell me about your business earlier?"

He closed the lid on the muffin container. "Before you saw the cottage on Anchor Lane, we didn't talk to each other very often."

"And when we did, I usually got all prickly." Paris sighed. "How do you find the time to look after the construction crews and run your own business?"

"It's hard, but I manage. When I started as site foreman at the tiny home village, I spent all my time managing the volunteers and paid staff. Now, another person does the day-to-day operations. I make sure the projects are on time and have the materials they need. Eventually, I'd like to work full time in my own business."

"Do you get paid for what you're doing at the cottages?"

Richard shook his head. "I didn't want to be paid. It's my way of giving back to the community."

Paris looked uncertainly at him. "Is that why you warned me about how difficult it is to start your own business?"

"It can consume your life. I was lucky. The church helped

me with childcare options, John let me use the old steamboat museum for my workshop, and I was able to borrow enough money to buy the wood I needed. Without everyone's support, I wouldn't still be in business."

"What's the hardest thing you've had to overcome?"

Richard frowned. She wouldn't want to open her flower shop if he told her everything. "I had to ask Shelley to be my accountant. The tax and financial side of owning a business drove me insane. The best thing I ever did was pay someone to build my website and automate my online ordering. It saves a lot of time."

"I don't know anything about setting up a website. Shelley suggested I talk to Emma Devlin."

"She helped me, too. Whatever she charges is worth it." He glanced at his watch before picking up his toolbox. "I'd better leave. Let me know if you have any issues with the next shelving units."

"I will. I'm glad you told me about your business."

With a nod, Richard stepped off the veranda and made his way around the side of the house. For two people who brought out the worst in each other, they were getting on too well. The cynical, battle-weary soldier inside of him knew their unspoken truce wouldn't last. But the man who'd made a new life for himself and his son hoped it did.

By Sunday afternoon, Paris was exhausted. The flowers they'd provided for the two weddings on Saturday were perfect and today's anniversary flowers were just as special. Despite working for most of the weekend, she'd returned to Blooming Lovely to double-check the flowers she needed to buy from tomorrow's market.

With no new online orders since Saturday afternoon, she

headed home. Andrea and her sons were meeting her for a walk around Flathead Lake. Later, she'd open a bottle of bubble bath and soak all her achy muscles away.

Mr. Riddley, her neighbor's overweight Golden Retriever, barked a friendly welcome as she parked her truck in the garage. She sent him a friendly wave before heading to the front door.

Reaching into her bag, she searched for her keys, then stopped. Sitting beside a container of daisies was a gift-wrapped parcel. A silver ribbon and large bow surrounded the bright red paper. It was pretty, festive, and so not hers.

Someone must have left it here by mistake. Her birthday wasn't for another six months and Christmas was even farther away. She picked up the gift. It was heavier than it looked.

She frowned when she saw her name on an envelope tucked under the ribbon. Looking over her shoulder, she searched the shaded front yard for Jackie or Andrea. It would be just like them to prank her with a booby-trapped gift. Holding it as far away as possible, she gave it a gentle shake to see if it exploded.

When a confetti fountain didn't erupt from the parcel, she sat on the veranda and opened the envelope. The hand-written message in bold letters made her frown. *A practical gift to last forever. Richard.*

While she was wondering why he'd left a present on her doorstep, her cell phone rang.

"Hello?"

"It's Richard. How are you?"

Panic made her breath catch. "Has something happened to the cottage?"

"It's fine. I left a gift for you on your veranda. I thought I'd better call to make sure you've seen it."

Paris looked at the pretty parcel. "I have. Work was super busy and I only arrived home a few minutes ago."

"Have you opened it?"

A silly, spine-tingling excitement made her smile. "Not yet. I'm sitting on the veranda wondering if it's safe to unwrap."

Richard sighed. "Why would I give you something that could hurt you?"

"I know you'd never do that. But you might want to scare me silly with a plastic snake or a big, hairy spider."

"Open the parcel, Paris."

His deep, sexy voice didn't help her spine-tingling moment. She must be more tired than she thought. If Andrea was right, Richard Dawkins didn't want to be anyone's Prince Charming.

"Paris?"

She jumped and nearly dropped the phone. "I'm here. I'll put you on speakerphone while I unwrap the box." The ribbon slipped off easily. "It's pretty paper."

"Jack helped me choose it."

Richard's muttered reply made her smile widen. "You're not blushing, are you?"

A sound halfway between a groan and a sigh carried on the still afternoon air. "Don't make me regret buying you a present."

Paris laughed. "I wouldn't dare. The last piece of tape is coming off now. I'm opening the paper." She frowned at the box sitting in her hands. If Richard *had* been blushing, it would be nothing compared to the heat rushing to her face.

"Are you still there, Paris?"

"I'm here. You bought me an electric drill?"

"It's a DeWalt 20-volt. The brushless motor gives you a longer run time on a single charge. I thought it would be better than using a screwdriver on your new shelving units."

Paris flicked the 'On' switch and smiled as the drill flared to life. "It's wonderful. Thank you."

"I'll give you a battery charger next week."

"You don't have to. I'll buy one."

"Paris?"

"Yes?"

"Just say thank you."

It was her time to sigh. "Thank you. I'll bake you some more muffins."

"You don't have to—"

"Just say thank you." She laughed when he didn't say anything.

Richard cleared his throat. "Thank you. There's a reason we didn't say more than a few words to each other before you saw the cottage."

She leaned against the front door. "There is?"

"We're both too stubborn to know what's good for us."

"Are you saying I'm good for you?" Paris clamped her hand over her mouth. "Sorry. I didn't mean to say that."

"I meant we're too stubborn to ask for help."

She held the drill against her chest. She'd turned a perfectly lovely moment into an awkward conversation they'd never get past.

Richard sighed. "But you could be right."

A slow smile replaced her frown. "Why am I good for you?"

"You make really good muffins. Jack and I could get used to them."

That wasn't what she thought he'd say. Her disappointment wasn't helped by Richard's gravelly laugh. "I thought you were going to say my unique fashion sense is rubbing off on you." *Liar*, she thought. But a girl had her dignity and she wasn't going to admit that she wanted to make a difference in his life.

"There isn't a lot of room for creativity in my wardrobe. I wear jeans and sweatshirts most of the time."

She wouldn't tell him he wore them very nicely. "You realize I can't resist a challenge, don't you?"

"I'd noticed."

How two little words could bring back the warm, fuzzy tingles so quickly was beyond her. "Do you want to be my next challenge?"

"I can't be anyone's challenge."

The sadness in his voice made her frown. "Why not?"

"I have issues."

If that was all he was worried about, she could put his mind at ease straightaway. "So do I."

"You're the most confident, assertive person I've ever met. What issues do you have?"

"Should I list them alphabetically or group them by subject?"

"I'm more of a numbers kind of guy."

Paris smiled. "I should have known, although comparing statistics can be unhealthy." Andrea waved at her from the sidewalk. "I have to go. Andrea's just arrived and we're going for a walk around the lake. Thanks again for the drill."

"You're welcome. Just ask if you want me to show you how to use it."

"I will. If you're home tomorrow night, I could drop off some muffins to you."

"Jack and I won't be at the village tomorrow night, but you can meet us at our new home."

"When did you move?"

Richard laughed. "We haven't moved yet. If Jack likes the house, I'll sign the sale and purchase agreement on Tuesday. I'll text you the address."

"That would be great."

"Enjoy your walk."

"I will. Bye." She ended the call and stared at the smile on Andrea's face. "It's not what you think."

Andrea leaned against the rail of the stairs. "When a woman has a dreamy look on her face, it can only mean one thing."

Paris turned on the drill. "It means I've found my 20-volt soulmate. Where are the boys?"

"Waiting for us at the lake."

Thankfully, Andrea didn't ask who she'd been speaking to. "All I have to do is fill my water bottle and then I'm ready."

"Take your time. The boys aren't in a hurry."

Paris hurried inside and left the drill on the kitchen table. She didn't know what issues Richard had, but she wanted to find out. If a fresh batch of muffins made it easier for him to talk, she'd take him some each night. And if he let her tweak his wardrobe, she'd be even happier.

CHAPTER 8

*R*ichard stepped out of his truck and stood beside Jack. The house he wanted to buy sat forlornly in front of them. With its blistering paint and overgrown garden, it could have been another vacation home waiting for someone to spruce it up.

"After we've mown the lawn, it will look better."

Jack lifted his head as his eyes roamed across the two-story building. "It's big."

Richard placed his arm around his son's shoulders. After living in a tiny home, any house would feel enormous. "The kitchen and living rooms are downstairs. Three bedrooms and a family bathroom are upstairs. Do you want to go inside?"

With a quick nod, Jack moved toward the gate. For someone who usually talked non-stop, his silence worried Richard. He thought they were both ready to move into their own home, but maybe he was wrong.

With a little jiggling, the front door swung open. "It needs to be painted, but we could do that later."

Jack stared at the floral wallpaper in the entryway. "It looks like Grandma's house."

Richard hadn't noticed the similarities, but he did now. His mom had opened up her kitchen and dining room, a lot like the owners of this house had done. Even the blue walls in the living room were something his mom could have chosen. "Grandma's house was probably built about the same time as this one. Do you want to see the bedrooms?"

Jack's freckles stood out against his pale skin. "Are you sure this will be our forever home?"

The unexpected question made Richard's heart sink. Jack hadn't wanted to leave his grandma's house in California. Coming to Montana had taken him away from the only stable home he'd known since Richard returned from Afghanistan.

"If you like it, it can be our forever home."

"I told Grandma we're looking at a house today. Is it still okay if she stays with us?"

"Of course, it is. But Grandma won't want to live here all the time. She has lots of friends in Los Angeles."

Jack sighed. "That's okay. She said she could make cookies with me and go for lots of walks. Can we take a photo of one of the bedrooms and send it to her?"

"She'd like that." Richard almost felt sorry for his mom. If Jack had his way, she would be living in Sapphire Bay by the end of the month.

While he was thinking about his mom, Jack was already walking toward the stairs. "If Grandma decided to live here, she could make new friends. Pastor John and Shelley have lots of programs at the church. And Alfie will like walking around the lake."

Alfie was Richard's mom's Cairn Terrier and the reason Jack wanted a dog. On a good day, Alfie reminded him of a miniature version of an Ewok from Star Wars. On a bad day, he was an overexcited, yappy dog who couldn't sit still.

"Grandma knows she can stay with us whenever she likes."

That seemed good enough for Jack. Without any encouragement, he bounded up the stairs and disappeared into one of the bedrooms. "This would be a great room for Grandma," he yelled from the first floor.

Richard made a mental note to call his mom tonight. If Jack suddenly asked her to live with them, she'd feel terrible saying no. At least this way, she could think of lots of great reasons why she needed to stay in Los Angeles.

"That's the room I was going to use. Have a look at the other two."

Jack hurried down the hallway. When Richard joined him in the last bedroom, his eyes were shining. "Grandma would like any of the rooms."

"I'm sure she would." Richard pulled back the lace curtains on the bedroom window. "You can't see Flathead Lake from here, but there's a great view of the mountains."

Jack looked around the bedroom and smiled. "When can we move in?"

Richard breathed a sigh of relief. "As soon as I pay the owner, we can leave the tiny home village."

"Does that mean we can look for a kitten at the animal shelter?"

"It does, but we won't adopt a kitten until we've moved all our things here. Do you want to see the swing in the apple tree?"

Jack didn't need a second invitation. He rushed downstairs and waited for Richard beside the doors overlooking the backyard.

Before they'd arrived, Richard was worried Jack wouldn't see the potential in the house. But potential meant nothing to his son. All he wanted was somewhere to call home. Somewhere that gave him more stability than the tiny home they were renting. And somewhere his grandma could stay.

PARIS PARKED her truck behind Richard's. The two-story home looked like the other vacation homes scattered throughout Sapphire Bay.

Most people with lake views had remodeled their homes. But others, like this one, were still waiting for someone to shower them with love and attention.

As she stepped onto the sidewalk, the sound of a young boy's laughter caught her attention. Instead of knocking on the front door, she made her way around the side of the house.

Beneath a large apple tree, Richard was pushing Jack on an old wooden swing. "Hi. That looks like fun."

"Hi, Paris," Jack said with a carefree smile. "Do you want a swing? Dad said it's safe."

"I'm okay. I'm not great with heights." Paris winced as Jack's legs touched the branches of the tree. If he fell, he could break his legs or worse. "I like the house."

"Dad said it needs to be painted and he's going to show me how to mow the lawns." With a leap that made Paris' heart pound, Jack launched himself off the swing and landed with a soft thud on the ground. "And we're getting a kitten, but not right away. Dad said we need to bring all our stuff here first."

"That makes sense. Your dad said you enjoyed the muffins I baked, so I've brought you some more." She held the container toward Jack. "They're banana chocolate chip with lemon frosting."

"Yum. Can I have one now?"

Richard ruffled Jack's hair. "Why don't we all have one on the veranda?"

"Like a picnic," Jack said enthusiastically.

While he raced ahead, Paris looked around the backyard. "The property is huge. How did you find it?"

"The owner asked Pastor John if he knew anyone who wanted to buy a fixer-upper. He thought of Jack and me."

"Did they realize how difficult it is to find houses that are for sale?"

"John recommended listing it with a realtor, but she was happy selling it through him. I'm glad she did. Otherwise, I wouldn't have stood a chance of buying it. After we've had something to eat, do you want to look inside?"

"I'd love to." She studied Richard's face. "You've cut your hair."

He lifted his hand, then dropped it to his side. "I thought I'd better tidy myself up. I'm seeing the lawyer in the morning."

She grinned at the blushing six-foot-five man in front of her. "You look very handsome."

"Thanks. I think. I like your dress, too."

Paris looked at the rainbow and unicorn print on her 1960s-inspired skirt. "I needed a pick-me-up this morning, so I chose my happy skirt."

"What happened?"

Telling Richard too much about her dysfunctional relationship with her mom would only make her feel worse.

"You don't have to tell me if you don't want to."

"It's okay. My mom called me last night. She isn't impressed with my decision to open a flower shop."

"Come on, Dad," Jack yelled from the veranda steps. "The muffins are ready."

"We're coming." He looked at Paris with a rueful smile. "If

you haven't guessed, Jack loves muffins. Why doesn't your mom think it's a good idea to open a flower shop?"

"She thinks I'll enjoy it for a year or two, then get bored."

"Is this part of the stickability thing you told me about?"

"It's more than that." She looked at the veranda. "Jack was serious about having a picnic." Richard's son had taken the paper napkins out of the box and opened them, covering enough of the wooden deck to accommodate three large muffins.

"It's the company he likes more than anything."

Paris blushed. "That's a nice thing to say, but I think the muffins have made the biggest impression." She joined Jack on the deck and grinned. "This looks great."

"Thanks. Do you want a muffin?"

"Yes, please."

With a flourish, Jack scooped one up and handed it to her. "This is going to be our house."

"You're really lucky. Have you chosen which bedroom you'll have?"

Jack took an enormous bite of his muffin and nodded. "Yep. Grandma's going to sleep in the room beside mine, but only when she visits."

"She must be excited."

Richard looked a little worried. "She is, but she had a similar reaction to your mom."

For some reason, that made her feel better. "Once she sees the house and where it's located, she'll want to visit as often as she can."

"Grandmas are the best people in the whole world," Jack said with pride.

Paris couldn't agree more. "My grandma would have liked coming here, too, but she died a few years ago."

"Do you think she can see what you're doing from heaven?"

Paris leaned toward him. "I have a feeling she sees everything, even the things I don't want her to know about."

"That's what Dad says about Mom. She went away when I was three, and now she's in heaven."

"I'm sorry." She glanced at Richard. It was difficult to know what was going through his mind.

"It's okay," Jack said quickly. "I didn't spend much time with her. When Dad was in the army, I lived with Grandma and Granddad."

Paris had no idea why he hadn't lived with his mom, but she knew what it was like to be raised by a grandparent. "Your grandma must have enjoyed spending time with you."

"She said I'm like dad, except I don't like broccoli or mushrooms."

Richard helped himself to a muffin. "Unlike my son, I eat anything."

"Dad's eaten worms and grasshoppers, and all kinds of bugs."

"Your dad's more adventurous than I am."

Richard wiped his hands on one of the napkins. "Since we're talking about being adventurous, did you bring the electric drill with you?"

"It's in my truck. I didn't know if you'd have time to show me how to use it."

"It won't take long." He looked at his watch and then at Paris. "Why don't you follow us to the old steamboat museum? I've got plenty of wood you can practice on."

"Can we show Paris the table you're making?" Jack asked excitedly.

"If she wants to see it, we can."

Paris smiled. "I'd love to see the table." When she lifted her eyes to Richard's, a silly tingle of awareness shot down her spine. "Thanks for inviting me."

"You're welcome. Are you ready to leave?"

She wrapped the rest of her muffin in a napkin and nodded. "I am now."

Jack ate his muffin in double-quick time and jumped to his feet. "Dad's workshop is great. I'll show you the special wood he uses for some of his furniture."

As they walked toward their trucks, Paris listened to Jack tell her more about the workshop. If it was half as good as he said, she couldn't wait to see it.

PARIS HAD DRIVEN past the old steamboat museum many times since she'd moved to Sapphire Bay, but she'd never been inside. It wasn't until she walked through the front door, that she realized how enormous the red-brick building was.

After passing a reception desk in the large foyer, Richard opened a set of double doors. Judging by what she saw, this must be the main workshop area. Five tiny homes in various stages of construction were dotted around the room.

"This is where we do most of the tiny home construction. Between fifteen and twenty people can be working on them at any given time."

She was surprised so many people were involved. "Are they volunteers or paid staff?"

"Both. The management team are paid. The students from the church's construction program help us three days a week as part of their work experience. By the end of the program, they've earned enough credits to buy a full set of tools. Other people from the community are treated as volunteers."

She stopped in front of one of the tiny homes. With its wide veranda, high-pitched roof, and gingerbread trim, it looked completely different from the ones in Sapphire Bay. "This house is bigger than the ones in the village."

"They were designed as accessible homes for people with disabilities. We're making them for a social housing development in Wyoming. Once they're finished, we'll start on another dozen homes that are going to Red Deer."

Paris was surprised at how popular the houses were. "You must be pleased that so many people want to buy them."

"We are. Without the profit from these homes, we wouldn't be able to build more tiny homes in Sapphire Bay or finance the wraparound support services. My workshop is over here." Richard pointed toward another set of doors at the back of the workshop.

Jack ran ahead of them. "Dad has a secret entrance outside, but it's locked after everyone goes home."

"It makes it safer when I'm working here with Jack," Richard explained.

Her eyes widened when she saw Richard's workshop. Although not as large as the area they'd walked through, it was still ten times bigger than she'd expected. "This is amazing."

"Most people are surprised by how big it is."

Jack stood beside a long rectangular table. "Dad's making this table for a lady in Polson."

Paris was impressed. "It looks wonderful. The top has a lovely grain."

"We rescued the wood from a barn on my client's ranch. It dates back to the early 1900s."

The sense of pride in his voice made her look differently at what was in the workshop. Apart from this table, another two sat beside it. Unlike this one, the others were a rich, deep brown and had bench seats tucked underneath.

"I'll finish those tables tomorrow. By Friday, they'll be shipped to their final destination."

Jack walked across to a wall of shelves. "Look at these boxes, Paris. We're going to sell them at the Christmas Markets."

She left her electric drill on a work table and joined Jack. When she saw the exquisite boxes that were inlaid with different colored wood, she sighed. "They're lovely. What wood are they made from?"

Richard stood beside them. "Hickory, American Oak, and Mahogany. Jack designs the final pattern."

From another shelf, Jack pulled off a box of small wooden shapes. "Like this."

Kneeling on the concrete floor, he tipped out some diamond-shaped blocks and created a star. "I can make crosses, stars, and if I use these ones"—he took some rectangular blocks out of another box—"I can make.." He looked up at his dad. "What's the 'H' word?"

"Herringbone."

"That's it. A herringbone pattern."

Richard handed Paris another beautiful box. "Each one is different. Jack helps me make them and we share the profits."

Jack scooped the blocks off the floor. "I'm saving my money for a new legos set."

She opened the lid and ran her fingers over the gleaming wood. "It's beautiful. How much are they?"

"It depends on the size and the time it takes to make them," Richard explained. "We'll sell that one for about seventy dollars."

"This is where we choose the special wood from." Jack showed Paris a set of heavy metal shelves toward the back of the room.

After she'd admired the different types of wood, Richard reached into a large container. "And these are my offcuts from the outdoor furniture. I'll show you how to use the electric drill using what's in here."

By the time Richard had shown her how to change the drill bits, alter the direction the drill rotated, and adjust the torque, she wondered if it would be easier to assemble the shelves using an old-fashioned screwdriver set.

"It's okay," Jack whispered. "I got confused when Dad showed me, too, but I'm good now. If you get stuck, I'll help."

"Thank you," she whispered back.

Richard frowned. "Have I made it too complicated?"

"I'm not very mechanically minded, but I like a challenge."

The former mountain man, who now had a city slicker haircut, picked up a handful of screws. "That's one of the things I like about you. You're happy to give anything a try." Holding two pieces of wood together at ninety degrees, he pointed to the edge where they met. "Connect a screw into the bit and drill it into here."

Paris held her breath as she concentrated on what she had to do. When the pointy end of the screw disappeared into the wood, she grinned. "It's easier than I thought."

"Try another one."

She added a second screw to the joint and then flipped the wood around. Richard handed her another offcut and she screwed it into place. By the time she was onto her fourth piece of wood, she was feeling more confident.

When Richard gave her a metal bracket, she picked up a shorter screw and changed the drill bit. "If I want a different career, I could join the volunteers who make the tiny homes."

"Don't consider that option too quickly," he said with a smile. "You have a flower shop to open in a few weeks."

Paris attached the bracket, then took an envelope out of her pocket. "While we're talking about my business, this is an invitation to the official opening of The Flower Cottage. It's on a Saturday morning so, hopefully, you and Jack can make it."

Richard read the handmade card. "We'll make sure we

can. I'm glad you chose the weekend after the cottage is supposed to be ready."

"Penny thought it was a good idea, too. If there are any last-minute issues, it gives everyone a few extra days to finish." She looked at the frame she'd made and smiled. "Thanks for taking the time to show me how to use the drill."

"If you have any problems, let me know. When are the shelving units arriving?"

"The supplier assured me they'll be here by the end of the week. Can I put them together in the cottage on Friday night?"

"I can't see why not. The walls will be painted by then and the floors should be polished and ready to go."

Paris picked up the drill. "I can't wait to see what everything looks like. I'd better leave you to enjoy the rest of the evening. I'll see you at this week's flower decorating class, Jack."

"Are we still making wreaths?"

She knew how much he was looking forward to this week's activity. "We are. Kylie has donated some pretty ribbon so you can hang the wreath when you get home."

Jack looked up at his dad. "Can we put it in our new house?"

"As soon as we move in, we can."

On that positive note, Paris said goodbye and walked back to her truck. After a lot of planning, she'd almost finished everything she had to do to open The Flower Cottage. She just hoped there were no unexpected surprises.

CHAPTER 9

*B*y Wednesday, Richard was busy managing the crew who were working on the next cottage in Anchor Lane. Unlike the first house, the roof on the second cottage needed to be completely replaced. Luckily, Penny had asked a builder to look at each cottage before work began, so they knew how much time it would take to do a complete remodel.

"Did someone check the invoice from the roofing supply company?" he asked Tommy.

"It's in the book with the other invoices."

Richard opened one of the folders he'd left onsite. With Paris's cottage almost finished, he was using her kitchen counter as a temporary workstation. By Friday evening, he'd take everything back to the old steamboat museum while they made the second cottage more weathertight.

"I've found it."

Tommy picked up a box of unused tiles. "Paris is here."

Richard looked up and studied the worried expression on her face. "What's happened?" He hadn't heard anything from her since Monday, so he presumed everything was going to plan.

"I tried calling you, but it kept going to voicemail."

He picked up his phone and frowned. "I turned off the ring tone during a meeting. That will be why I haven't had any interruptions this afternoon. How can I help?"

"Do you remember me telling you about the couple getting married in April?"

"The ones who'll be your first major clients?"

Paris nodded. "They were originally getting married at the end of April, but the bride's sister has to return to Australia earlier than she thought. They've brought their wedding forward to the last Saturday in March."

"That's the same day you're opening The Flower Cottage."

"It is. They aren't getting married until four o'clock, but I don't know how I'll welcome customers to my shop and organize the flowers for Nadine and Carl's wedding. They've chosen some big, over-the-top arrangements that will take me days to create."

"Can Kylie and Jackie help?"

"Kylie has to work fewer hours because of her pregnancy, so I don't like asking her. Jackie will help if she can, but she's busy at Blooming Lovely. Do you know anyone in the construction program who would be interested in building the frames I'll need?"

"I'll ask, but they're already working on these cottages and the tiny homes. If no one's available, I could make them."

"Are you sure you have the time?"

Richard knew he didn't, but that wouldn't stop him from helping her. "If I do it, I'll have to start this weekend. Do you have somewhere you can store them?"

Paris nodded. "I have plenty of spare room in my garage. Nadine sent me some photos of the type of wedding arches she wants. The design she chose shouldn't take too long to build."

He took the folder she handed to him and looked at the images. "They're getting married outside?"

"That's changed, too. It will be too cold to get married in Nadine's parents' garden, so they're using a friend's barn. The five rectangular frames will be covered in flowers and placed along a path leading to the barn. They have to be high enough for everyone to walk under." She pointed to the photos. "Nadine wants them to look like this."

Richard studied the wooden frames supporting the large floral arrangements. "The flowers will have to be carefully balanced. Otherwise, the frame could tip over."

"I thought I could add some posts to the left-hand side to provide more stability."

"It would spoil the floating effect they probably want."

"I was worried about that, too. But, as long as the posts match the material we're using for the rest of the frames, Nadine said it was okay."

"That's good." After looking at each picture, he knew why Paris was worried. Preparing for the opening of her business was bad enough. Creating over-the-top flower arrangements at the same time was asking for trouble. "I'll text the apprentices in our programs and let you know if anyone can help."

"Thanks. I know I'll be running against time to finish everything before the wedding, but it's important. Nadine's mom knows a lot of influential people. If she posts great reviews about the flowers on her social media accounts, I'll have more work than I'll know what to do with. But, if something goes wrong, I could be out of business."

She must be exaggerating. "Are you sure?"

Paris slipped the folder into her bag. "Nadine's surname is Kingston. Her dad owns half of Montana."

"As in the property tycoon, Tom Kingston?"

"That's him. The wedding guest list is a who's who of *Fortune* 500 executives and television personalities."

Richard didn't keep up to date on a lot of things that happened around Sapphire Bay, but even he'd heard of the Kingston family. "This is too important to leave to the apprentices. I'll start building the frames tomorrow night. We can store them in my workshop until you need them."

Paris smiled and then threw her arms around his neck, hugging him tightly. "Thank you. You don't know how much this means to me."

Before he'd figured out what to do with his hands, she'd already stepped away. "I'll make you and Jack dinner on the days you're helping me. And, whether you want my money or not, I'm paying you."

"That's not necessary. I'm happy to—"

Paris put her hands over her ears. "I'm not listening. I'm getting paid to provide the flowers for the wedding. I couldn't make the bride and groom's dreams come true on my own, so you deserve to be paid for what you're doing."

Richard sighed. The stubborn tilt to her chin told him she wouldn't take no for an answer. "Fine. I'll send you a bill for the cost of the materials."

"And I'll add on some money for your labor. If there's anything else you need, just ask." Like a whirlwind gathering speed, she collected her bag and waved goodbye to Tommy. "I have to get back to Blooming Lovely. We're working late tonight."

"Good luck."

"Thanks. I forgot to ask about your house. Were you able to buy it?"

"I was. You're looking at the proud owner of a new mortgage."

Paris' wide smile made his heart pound. "That's fantastic.

I can help you move on any day except the Saturday I'm opening The Flower Cottage."

"Jack and I can manage."

"I'm sure you can, but it's my turn to help you."

With those words ringing in his ears, Paris sent him another smile and hurried out of the room.

Tommy collected a box of tile offcuts. "Is she always like that?"

Richard picked up his clipboard. "It looks like it." Too late, he remembered Paris still had the drawings of the frames in her bag. Not that it mattered. After Jack finished at The Welcome Center's writing club, he'd drop into Blooming Lovely and borrow the folder.

As long as he placed the timber order by eight o'clock tomorrow, he'd have the supplies by the afternoon. And, if luck were on his side, the frames would go together faster than he thought.

PARIS CLICKED another screw onto the electric drill and followed what Richard had done. So far, they'd finished three of the frames for Nadine's wedding. "It's just as well you changed the design. I wouldn't have made the frames this big."

Richard lifted a long piece of wood onto the drop cloth he was using. "If they were less than seven feet high, the guests' heads could hit the flowers as they walk under them."

Jack brought his paint bucket across to his dad. "Could you pour more undercoat into my bucket?"

"Sure. You're doing a great job."

Standing a little taller, Jack grinned at Paris. "I like painting."

"I can tell. There isn't one drip mark anywhere." Jack was

painting the frame for his new bed. If he followed the drawing he'd shown her, the old wooden frame would eventually be bright blue with pictures of fish and dolphins across the headboard.

Richard carried the bucket of undercoat to where Jack was working. "Here you go. Let me know if you need help."

"I will."

Paris measured another length of wood. "I'm borrowing Kylie's truck when I collect the first order of flowers for the wedding."

"Will that hold them all?"

"I think so. I split the order into two to make it easier to keep the flowers fresh." Taking the pencil out of her tool belt, she marked where the wood needed to be cut. Richard stood beside her, waiting to put it through the saw. She felt his nearness like prickles brushing against her skin. "Measure twice and cut once?"

"You're learning."

His deep, sexy voice made her sigh. She was learning more than carpentry skills. At the rate she was going, Jackie would need to have a stern talk with her about sticking to her life plan. And nowhere, not even in the fine print, did it mention falling for a man with a more complicated life than hers.

Lifting one end of the wood, she helped Richard carry it across to the saw. "I spoke to Pastor John today. He said he's looking forward to seeing you on Friday."

Richard dropped his safety glasses over his eyes. "I bet he is. He cleaned me out of chips at our last poker game."

"You play poker?"

His slow smile made Paris' toes curl. "Only on a good night. The rest of the time, I'm an easy target for Wyatt and Ethan."

Jack grinned. "Dad said he doesn't have a good poker face."

Paris' eyebrows rose. Of all the people in Sapphire Bay, he seemed the best at keeping his thoughts to himself.

Richard cut the piece of wood. "My friends have known me a lot longer than you have."

The softly spoken words made her frown. "How did you—"

"You can't hide what you're thinking." Richard tapped the end of her nose. "That's a compliment, not an insult. Help me carry this post to your work area."

Paris sighed. It was just as well they'd have the frames finished tonight. Otherwise, she'd be in danger of liking him more than she should.

Kneeling on the floor, she screwed the legs of the frame into place. Richard helped her flip the arch over so she could do the same on the other side.

"Your phone's ringing, Paris."

"Thanks, Jack." She walked across to her jacket and pulled her cell phone out of her pocket. When she saw who was calling, she almost let it go to voicemail. "Hi, Mom."

"Darling, it's so good to hear your voice. Cynthia just told me you're opening your flower shop in a couple of weeks. Why didn't you tell me it's so soon?"

The only time her mom called her darling was when she'd been drinking. Paris' only consolation was that by the morning, Donna wouldn't remember anything they'd talked about. "Aunt Cynthia called when I was choosing some shelving for the store. We started talking and one thing led to another."

"Well, I'm very proud of you. I always knew you'd make something of yourself."

Paris rubbed her forehead. Her mom was definitely drunk. "Where are you?"

"I'm in Las Vegas with Jerry. He was invited to a high-stakes game and we couldn't say no."

"What about your job?"

The silence on the end of the phone told Paris the answer to her question. "How long have you been out of work?"

"I don't know why you always think the worst of me. I'm still working for Callagher and Mitchem, although sometimes I wonder why I bother. They never listen to any of my ideas for improving our processes. But, as Jerry says, my salary pays the bills."

Considering Jerry's only income came from the casino circuit, Paris figured they needed some kind of regular income.

"I was thinking of flying to Sapphire Bay. Jerry has a couple of weeks off before his next tournament. We could be there for the opening of the store and meet your friends."

Paris' heart plummeted. "It's not a good time. I'm really busy."

"I could help. It would be just like old times."

Remembering those times made Paris' stomach churn. "It's better if you stay home. Your boss will appreciate you coming back to work after you've been away."

"He doesn't appreciate anything I do."

As her mom told her what was happening at work, Paris glanced at Richard. He was kneeling on the ground, screwing another frame together. Anyone listening to the one-sided conversation would wonder what was going on. Most people enjoyed talking to their mom but, for her, it was a minefield.

"I have to go, Mom. Thanks for calling."

"Don't you want to hear about Jerry's birthday? We had such a good time. Cynthia and Dave flew down from Seattle and spent the weekend with us."

Paris had heard all about the forty-eight-hour celebration that had ended in the fountain outside the Bellagio Resort.

Her mom was lucky she hadn't drowned. "Aunt Cynthia told me about it. I'll call you next week."

"But I really want to see you, darling. We never spend time together."

"We'll talk about it next week. Bye, Mom." Before Donna could say anything, Paris ended the call. With trembling hands, she turned off her phone and left it on the table.

Richard placed some pieces of wood beside the frame she was making. "Are you all right?"

"I'm fine." Taking a deep breath, she focused on what she was here to do. "After I've attached the corner braces, I'll make the supports for the legs." She picked up her drill, looked at Richard, and wished she hadn't. There was an understanding in his eyes that made her heart ache.

Instead of asking more questions, he pointed to the wood he'd left on the floor. "I've cut the wood you'll need for the bottom of the frames."

"Thanks." It wasn't until she was halfway through attaching the first corner brace that she realized there were tears in her eyes. So much for being a confident, mature adult. Beneath her colorful clothes and forced smile was a scared ten-year-old, hoping her mom didn't suddenly arrive and show everyone why Paris never spoke about her.

CHAPTER 10

*L*ater that week, Paris looked around the meeting room at The Welcome Center. Nine eager students were creating gorgeous wreaths.

Jack must have been planning what he'd make since their last class. The drawing he'd brought with him was far more complicated than the other designs she'd seen. "Good job, Jack. I like the way you're using the foam balls."

"The blue one is earth and the silver one is the moon. It's sparkly because it's surrounded by stars."

Nora, Jack's friend, looked up from the pink and purple wreath she was making. "What's your favorite star?"

"Sirius 'cos it's the brightest one in the sky."

"How come you know lots about the stars and planets?" Charlie, Jack's other friend, asked.

"When I lived with Grandma, she told me all kinds of things about them."

"My grandma died," Nora said sadly.

"You can spend time with mine, if you like." Jack leaned forward and whispered across the table. "She's coming to visit as soon as we move into our new house."

That set off a whole new set of questions about Jack's house. Before the children became too distracted, Paris checked the time. "Your parents will be here in ten minutes and it would be good to have finished your wreaths. Does anyone need more glitter?"

Nora waved a pink daisy in the air. "Can I have some, please?"

"Of course, you can. What about you, Charlie?"

"No, thanks. I don't like glitter."

Unlike Jack's wreath, Charlie's was a spontaneous burst of color. He must have used every type of flower Paris had brought to the class. The other children's wreaths were completely different, but just as lovely. "Who's ready for their ribbon?"

Four hands shot in the air. "Me!" they said excitedly.

After the first set of wreaths were finished, the next group of children were ready for their ribbons. By the time Paris tied Jack's to the back of his wreath, he could hardly contain his excitement.

"Dad will think this is so awesome."

"You've done a wonderful job." She looked around the room and smiled. "All we have to do is clean up." A series of groans filled the air. "It's not that bad. The people on Jack's table can collect the leftover flowers and leaves, and put them in the buckets. Annie and Desiree can collect all the glitter containers, and everyone else can throw the rubbish away. You've got three minutes."

In a flurry of activity, everyone cleaned what they could in double-quick time. Paris would have to stay behind to vacuum, but she didn't mind. Everyone had enjoyed the class, even if it looked like a glitter bomb had exploded inside the room.

"Okay. If your parent or caregiver is waiting outside, you

can leave the room. Otherwise, stay with me." Everyone's head turned toward the large window facing the corridor. One after another, the children picked up their wreaths and said goodbye.

When Richard appeared in the doorway, he smiled. "It looks as though you've had a busy afternoon."

Paris stacked the last chair with the others and returned his smile. "It was fun."

"Look at my wreath." Jack showed his dad what he'd made. "The blue ball in the center is the earth and the silver ball is the moon. I painted the leaves blue like the ocean and the flowers are the fish."

"I'm impressed. We'll have to take a photo and send it to Grandma."

"Can we do it now? Paris could be in the photo, too. Grandma would like to see her."

Paris shook her head. "I don't need to be in the picture. How about I take a photo of you and your dad with the wreath?"

Richard pulled out his cell phone. "I like Jack's idea better." When Paris didn't move, he sent her an amused glance. "Are you camera shy?"

There were so many ways she could have answered that question, but none of them involved the camera. "Your mom doesn't know me."

"I told Grandma about you," Jack said quickly. "She said our flower arranging class sounds like something she'd enjoy."

Paris looked into Jack's expectant face and sighed. "Okay. Just one photo."

Wasting no time, Richard placed a chair beside Jack. "Stand on here. I'll take the photo before Paris changes her mind."

"I won't do that," she muttered.

Jack handed his dad the wreath while he climbed onto the chair. "I'm ready."

Richard held his phone in front of them. "We need to huddle closer."

Paris stepped closer to Jack and smiled at the camera.

After Richard took the photo, he showed it to her.

"It's great." She was glad everyone had their eyes open and smiles on their faces. With his wreath in front of him, Jack looked incredibly proud. She only hoped Richard's mom didn't think she was more than a family friend.

A noise coming down the hallway was just the distraction she needed.

Shelley appeared in the doorway with a vacuum cleaner. When she saw Paris, she grinned. "Who needs a yellow brick road when you have a path of glitter?"

"You don't need to do the vacuuming," Paris told her. "I can do it."

"Don't be silly. I'm happy to help. It's just as well I didn't bring Toto with me. He's such a bouncy puppy that he'd be covered in sparkles, too."

"You have a puppy?" Jack looked at Shelley with eyes that were as wide as saucers.

Shelley nodded. "We picked him up from the animal shelter last weekend. The first person we introduced him to was Paris."

"I was wearing my Dorothy costume from *The Wizard of Oz*, and he loved it. That's when Pastor John and Shelley decided to call him Toto."

Jack ran to the doorway and looked down the corridor. "Can I see him?"

Shelley glanced at Richard before replying. As soon as he nodded, she handed Paris the vacuum cleaner. "It's all yours. I have another introduction to do."

Jack looked at his dad. "Do you want to come?"

"I'll join you after I've helped Paris clean the rest of the room."

She opened her mouth to say he didn't need to do that, but Shelley spoke first.

"What a good idea." She rested her arm across Jack's shoulders. "I hope you like wiggly puppies?"

"I love all kinds of puppies."

His wistful reply made Paris smile. If his reaction to Toto was as besotted as hers, he wouldn't want to leave Shelley's office.

AFTER JACK AND SHELLEY LEFT, Richard put away the chair they'd used. "On a scale of one to ten, how cute is Toto?"

Paris rolled a plastic tablecloth into a ball. "If ten is as cute as apple pie, he's a twenty."

Richard was worried she'd say that. "I promised Jack we'd get a kitten after we move into our new house, but he really wants a puppy."

"He might change his mind when he sees a kitten he likes."

"I hope so, but he grew up with my parents' dog. Marley never left Jack's side."

"That sounds like a wonderful friendship. How long did you and Jack live with your parents?"

He glanced at Paris before throwing some green foliage in the garbage bag. It was the type of question most people would ask, but that didn't mean he was comfortable answering it. "Jack lived with my parents for ten months before I came home from my last tour of duty. We stayed with them for a couple of years after that. Dad died last year."

"I'm sorry."

"It's okay. He was diagnosed with terminal cancer in

January. By then, it was too late for treatment. He died peacefully in the local hospice a few months later."

"That must have been hard."

Richard swallowed the knot of grief in his throat. "It was. I don't know how Mom coped with everything, but she did."

"Can I ask you a personal question?"

His eyebrows rose. "You mean all the other questions weren't personal?"

"I'm not that bad," she muttered.

She looked so worried that he smiled. "It's just as well I'm used to your inquisitive mind. Ask me anything. If I don't want to answer, I'll tell you."

"Other than what you've told me about your parents, you don't talk about your life before you came to Sapphire Bay. Why?"

He picked up the vacuum cleaner. "Because it isn't interesting."

"It might be." Paris frowned. "How long were you in the army?"

"Six years. I was honorably discharged after I lost my leg in Afghanistan."

"That must have been traumatic."

Richard took a deep breath. "I had two years of operations, intense physical therapy, and counseling. At the end, I was still messed up."

"Is that when you decided to move to Sapphire Bay?"

"I thought you were only asking one question?"

Paris' impish smile dissolved some of his mounting panic. "I was making the most of our time alone. I won't tell anyone what you've said."

"It's not top secret. I didn't come to Sapphire Bay for the scenery or the fishing. I came here because of Pastor John. A friend started going to John's PTSD support group. He'd already gone through the usual counseling sessions, but he was still struggling. Within six months of talking to John and the rest of the group, he felt better."

"What makes John's group different?"

Richard helped Paris move a table. "We usually have a meal together and talk about things that don't involve PTSD. When someone's struggling, we listen and try to help. Pastor John has been where we are. He knows what it feels like to return to a life that's the same but different."

"I'm glad you found him."

"So am I." He thought about his journey to Montana—the doubt and fear that had followed him every step of the way. "I was terrified I was doing the wrong thing. My parents wanted me to leave Jack with them, but I couldn't. I'd already lost my wife because of who I'd become. If I had to leave Jack behind, I wouldn't have made it to Sapphire Bay."

Paris' eyes widened. "Are you saying—"

"Without Jack, my life wasn't worth living. He was the reason I got out of bed each morning. Because of him, I wanted to be a better person. When we arrived here, all we had were a few suitcases and my truck. John found a room for us in The Welcome Center and encouraged Jack to join the children's programs. I volunteered at the church. When John discovered I had construction experience, he sent me to the old steamboat museum to help build the tiny homes."

"And look at you now."

Paris' gentle smile made his heart pound. "Yeah. Covered in glitter and hoping my son doesn't fall in love with a puppy."

"At least Toto won't be going home with you."

Richard wouldn't put anything past his son or Pastor John. "When John realizes Jack loves puppies, he'll ask him to babysit Toto when he goes out with Shelley."

Paris laughed. "That sounds like something he'd do. Especially if he thinks you have a soft spot for puppies."

Richard heard Jack's excited voice before he saw him. "We're about to be ambushed."

"It's too late for me," Paris said. "Toto's already won me over."

"Dad! Look who I've brought to say hello."

Attached to a bright red lead was the scruffiest ball of fur Richard had ever seen. With big, round eyes, a pink nose, and sticky-up ears, Toto was the cutest puppy he'd ever seen.

"Isn't he perfect?" Paris whispered.

Richard sighed. Almost as perfect as the woman beside him.

Jack picked up Toto and cuddled him close. "We played fetch, but Toto isn't too good at bringing the ball back."

Shelley grinned. "He's still more interested in eating everything."

"Pastor John said he'll be better when he's older." Jack patted Toto's head. "Do you want to hold him, Dad?"

Richard saw the pleading look in his son's eyes. "I'd love to, but we're not getting a puppy from the animal shelter."

"I know. Pastor John and Shelley said I can visit Toto whenever I like." Carefully, he handed the happy puppy to Richard. "You have to make sure you don't drop him," Jack warned. "He's only little and it might hurt him."

"I'll make sure he's okay." Richard held the puppy close to his chest and glanced at Paris. She looked just as besotted as Jack.

If he wasn't careful, Toto's big brown eyes might lull him into believing a puppy would make their family complete. Especially if it inspired Paris to visit them more often.

CHAPTER 11

*P*aris ran her finger down the sheet of instructions for the first shelving unit. With a silent prayer, she attached the screw to the end of the drill and pulled the trigger. With a whir, it disappeared into the frame.

"That's awesome," Jackie said from beside her. "If I'd known how good you are, I would have called you about my closet. The shelf brackets need to be tightened."

Andrea unpacked another shelving unit. "Before you say you'll help, I have a set of bookshelves I need to make. I'll barter endless cups of coffee and hot muffins for your expertise."

Paris grinned. "By the end of today, you won't need my help. If I can learn how to use an electric drill, you can, too."

"That might be a little optimistic," Jackie said as she handed Paris another screw. "My last boyfriend showed me how to use a drill, but I cross-threaded everything."

"All it takes is practice." Paris finished the top shelf, then handed Jackie the drill. "I'll hold the next shelf in place. Keep the drill level and gently push it toward the frame. The motor and screw will do the rest of the work."

"What if I damage the frame?"

Andrea hunted in a large container behind her. "If you're worried, practice on this piece of wood."

Paris handed her friend a screw. "There's a little magnet on the end of the drill bit. It keeps the screw in place while you're working out where it needs to go."

Jackie clicked the screw into place. After a few more instructions, the screw slid into the piece of wood. "I can't believe I did it."

"You can do anything," Paris reminded her. With a little more coaxing, Jackie tested her newfound construction skills on a shelving unit.

After it was finished, Andrea and Jackie moved the unit into the left-hand side of The Flower Cottage.

"One down, four to go," Paris said softly. "It looks great."

Jackie nodded. "I still can't believe Richard bought you an electric drill. Who does that?"

"Someone who's extremely practical and likes the person they're giving it to," Andrea said with a grin.

"Or someone with ulterior motives." Paris handed Andrea the drill. "Richard bought a house that needs a lot of work."

"I heard about that." Andrea studied the shelving unit sitting in pieces on the floor. "Here goes nothing." Within a few minutes, she had the first shelf attached to the frame. "Andy and Charlie wanted me to buy an electric drill when we moved into our house. But I thought my handy-dandy screwdriver was good enough."

"And now?" Jackie asked.

"I know why they wanted one." Andrea took the next shelf from Paris. "Mabel Terry said you've been spending a lot of time with Richard."

Paris sighed. "I can't believe you'd listen to anything she says. Mabel has a heart of gold, but she's a terrible gossip."

"She's also right. You *have* spent a lot of time with

Richard." Jackie took some pretty glass vases out of a box. "As well as teaching you how to use the drill, he's shown you his new home and helped make the frames for the wedding you're decorating."

"He's a nice person."

Andrea opened the next box of brackets. "Nice people don't always go out of their way to help others. Jack seems to like you, too."

Paris' eyes narrowed. "Jack's eight years old. He likes everyone. We need to focus on the shelving and not on Richard and his son."

"But it's more enjoyable talking about a potential boyfriend. Especially when none of us have dated anyone since we arrived in Sapphire Bay. Where would you like these vases?"

"On the first shelving unit," Paris told Jackie. "They're hand-blown glass. A lady in Red Deer made them."

"They're cute. So, when are you seeing Richard again?"

"I'm not—"

Andrea waved the drill in the air. "Yes, you are. He's everything you told me you need."

"Is that the list that includes someone who appreciates caramel brittle ice cream, foot massages, and Christmas carols sung in the snow?"

"And the ability to make you laugh," Andrea added. "From what I've heard, Richard ticks all your 'must have' boxes."

"He might come close, but I don't have time to date anyone."

Jackie placed the last vase on a shelf. "That's what you always say. Sometimes, you have to make the time. Is there anything else that needs unpacking?"

Paris took another box off the kitchen counter. "These wooden carvings need to go on the next set of shelves."

Andrea screwed another bracket into place. "What you're

doing here is great. It isn't easy finding places that will sell your products if you're a small business."

Carefully, Paris carried the box of sculptures across to Jackie. "Nate Milligan made these."

"Shona's son?" Jackie wiped down the table she was using as a workbench. When she saw the ornate candle holders, she smiled. "He's so talented. Kylie said the decorations he makes for the Christmas Shop sell out as soon as they appear in their catalog."

"I wonder if he'll come back to Sapphire Bay after he's finished college."

Paris helped Andrea with the next shelf. "Why wouldn't he?"

"There are lots of reasons. As well as not having many jobs, we don't have any of the things a large city can offer people."

"You came here with your boys."

"I had a good reason."

Even though Paris knew why she'd fled to Sapphire Bay, it still made her feel sad when she thought about Andrea's life. "I don't know whether Nate will come back but, if he does, he could start his own business."

"Just like you," Andrea said proudly. "My boys haven't stopped talking about your store."

Paris looked around the beautiful room. She was so proud of what she'd achieved, but it would all be for nothing if she didn't make a profit. "All I can think about is what could go wrong."

Andrea sent her a sharp glance. "Ignore those feelings. Even if something doesn't go according to plan, it doesn't matter."

Jackie helped lift another shelving unit into the sales area. "I second what Andrea said. Think positive thoughts."

That was easier said than done. Especially when she had less than a week to get everything ready.

Thanks to Richard and his team, the cottage was nearly ready and she had everything she'd ever imagined. Now all she had to do was find more customers.

RICHARD THREW his cards into the center of the table, happy to let Wyatt continue his winning poker streak without him.

"I can't believe you won another game," Ethan muttered from the other side of the table. "There should be a rule that says you can't win more than three games in a row."

Wyatt scooped up the mound of chips in front of him. "It must be my lucky night."

Pastor John scoffed. "There's nothing lucky about it. Are you sure you weren't born in Las Vegas?"

"I blame my uncanny ability to win on my grandfather."

Richard picked up his drink. "Was he a professional poker player?"

"Nope. A gardener. But when he wasn't working, he earned extra money in the back rooms of Atlantic City."

"I knew it," Ethan said disgustedly. "You've been genetically engineered to win."

Wyatt grinned. "I'll take any advantage I can get. Especially after John cleaned me out last week."

"That was divine intervention." John grabbed a handful of peanuts. "Unfortunately, no one's listening tonight."

As the banter continued around him, Richard's mind wandered over what was happening next week. In between making sure the construction crew had everything they needed for the second cottage on Anchor Lane, he had to finish two furniture orders and go to the opening of Paris' store.

He just hoped she was ready for the wedding she was decorating and the customers who'd be lining up to work with her.

"Earth to Richard. Where are you?"

He looked at his friend, Ben. He was the owner of the only Christmas tree farm in Sapphire Bay. "Sorry. I was thinking about something else. What did you say?"

"I asked about Paris. Is she happy with how her new store has turned out?"

Ethan groaned. "It's bad luck to mention anything about work on poker night."

John shuffled the cards. "It depends on whether Richard wants to talk about the cottages or Paris."

Wyatt frowned. "Why would he talk about..." He saw the blush heating Richard's face and frowned. "Am I missing something?"

"No."

John's eyebrows rose. "That's not what Jack said."

That didn't surprise Richard. Jack hadn't stopped talking about Paris, especially after they'd helped make the frames for next weekend's wedding. "What did he say?"

"He asked if Paris is your girlfriend."

Richard almost dropped his drink. "Why would he ask that?"

"You've hardly spoken to any single females in the last four years," John said with a grin.

"And you never take anyone to your workshop," Ethan added.

"It's not like I took her there on a date," Richard muttered. "We made frames for a wedding she's decorating." He didn't like the gleam in Ethan and John's eyes.

Wyatt looked as though he was catching up with everyone else's conspiracy theories. "But you did invite her to your new house."

"How did you—?"

"Penny told me. Paris said it's amazing."

A warm, fuzzy feeling settled in Richard's chest. He really needed to get a grip. One woman's opinion of his new home shouldn't make him grin like an idiot. But it wasn't one woman's. It was Paris'. And that mattered more than most.

John dealt the cards. "Is anyone helping Paris when she opens The Flower Cottage?"

"Two of the students she tutored at The Welcome Center will be there."

Ben glanced at his cards. "Kylie and Jackie are helping with the wedding she's decorating, too. They're taking the flowers to the barn and making sure everything's perfect. After The Flower Cottage closes, Paris will double-check the wedding venue and stay there until the bride and groom leave the reception." Ben looked at his friends' surprised faces. "What?"

Ethan looked at his cards and placed three chips in front of him. "I'll raise the bid to three bucks. How come you know so much about Paris' business?"

"Kylie hasn't talked about anything else for the last couple of weeks. She's as excited as Paris about the new store." With a heartfelt sigh, Ben dropped his cards into the center of the table. "I'm out."

Richard checked his cards. At least they were better than the last round. "I'll call."

Wyatt grinned. "I'm in. It looks as though we have a good round ahead of us."

"If that's code for more money coming your way, you might want to think again." Ben reached for another drink. "I have a feeling Richard's about to break your winning streak."

Richard frowned. "What gave you that idea?"

"You always play better when you're not overthinking the game. Paris is the perfect distraction."

Everyone's gaze honed in on Richard.

"Is this the beginning of something interesting in your life?" John asked.

"I don't have time for anything interesting," he mumbled. Although the same thought had gone through his head. Too many times. "And even if I did, I wouldn't know where to start. I haven't dated anyone since college."

Wyatt held up his hand when everyone started talking at once. "We're in the middle of a game. Hold off on the relationship advice until we're finished."

While John and Ethan told Wyatt what they thought of his plan, Richard breathed a sigh of relief. Hopefully, by the time this round was over, no one would care about his issues.

And if he believed that, he was seriously delusional.

CHAPTER 12

*F*or the first time since she'd decided to rent the cottage on Anchor Lane, Paris was really stressed. Even the bidding at this morning's flower market felt more strained. She didn't know whether it was her or if everyone was feeling the pressure of too many weddings and not enough staff.

Opening a flower shop in the middle of all the craziness wasn't helping. The people she regularly met at the market gave her lots of advice and good wishes, but that didn't help the weight sitting on her shoulders.

By the time she opened the back door of Blooming Lovely, she was sure something catastrophic was going to happen. She frowned when she saw Jackie. "Hi. You're early."

"I saw how many online orders were placed yesterday. I figured if I couldn't sleep, I might as well come into work. You're back earlier than usual, too."

"All the flowers we wanted were auctioned first. I was glad to leave."

Jackie glanced at her before reaching for another rose. "That's not like you."

Paris slid the first flower box into the refrigerator. "I'm worried about Saturday. I still have to make half the displays for The Flower Cottage, and Mrs. Kingston called. She wants to change the table centerpieces."

"She can't do that. Her daughter's wedding is in five days."

"I told her it would be impossible to find the crystal vases she wants, but she'd already found a supplier."

"That sounds like her." Jackie placed the bouquet she'd made in a special vase and ticked the order off their list. "Will the flowers you chose work with the new centerpieces?"

"I hope so. The company are fast-tracking a sample vase to me. I bought some extra flowers at the market to see if I can make it work. I'll be back soon."

Jackie followed Paris outside and picked up two boxes. "Whatever you do will look amazing. Once you've settled on a design, take a picture of it. That way, it will be easier to recreate it when we're making the actual centerpieces."

Paris turned to her friend. She was so overwhelmed with gratitude that tears stung her eyes. "You're already helping with the barn. Are you sure you can help with the centerpieces?"

"Of course, I can, and so will Kylie. We'll meet you at The Flower Cottage after work on Thursday. If they take longer than we think to make, Doris and Andrea won't mind being on standby. They enjoyed your flower arranging classes and said they'd help, too."

"I don't know what to say."

"We know how busy you are, so there's no need to say anything."

"I'll owe everyone dinner after the weekend's over. I'm just grateful Nadine isn't getting married until four o'clock."

Jackie grinned. "I'm surprised her mom hasn't changed the time of the wedding, too."

"Shh," Paris whispered. "She might hear you and think it's a great idea."

"And no one wants that." Jackie carried her flowers inside.

After she'd left, Paris took a moment to appreciate the quiet serenity of the morning. She'd worked hard all weekend, creating satin-wrapped frames for the display panels in her store, spraying ornate metal tables with white paint, ordering more business cards, and booking newspaper advertising for next weekend.

Tomorrow would be her last day at Blooming Lovely. From Wednesday, she was completely focused on Nadine's wedding and getting The Flower Cottage ready for the grand opening. Regardless of what Andrea and Jackie had said, she was terrified something would go wrong.

"Do you need a hand with the rest of the flowers?" Jackie asked from the back door.

Shaking her doom and gloom away, Paris forced a smile. "I can manage. I'll bring them in now."

Grabbing the boxes, she took them straight to the refrigerator. "Have you made the Donaldson's flower arrangement?"

Jackie checked the list of orders. "Not yet. You'll need four of the lilies you bought at the market."

While Paris organized the flowers, Jackie took some roses out of another box and placed them on a sheet of sparkly paper. "I saw Richard and Jack yesterday."

"You did?"

"I promised Shelley I'd take some cookies into the church after John's service. Richard and Jack were playing basketball with some other dads and their children."

Paris smiled. "I bet Jack enjoyed that. He loves playing basketball."

"Richard asked how you were doing."

"He did?"

"Yep. And if the glow on your face is anything to go by, you're equally interested in him."

"I'm not interested in that way. He's my friend." She picked up the clipboard, hoping Jackie got the hint and talked about something else.

"Remember what I said the other day. Step out of your comfort zone and make opportunities happen."

If Richard knew Jackie saw him as an opportunity, he'd be mortified. "I've pushed my comfort zone enough with The Flower Cottage."

Jackie studied Paris' flushed face. "I've known you for as long as you've lived in Sapphire Bay. What's the one thing you've always said you want?"

"To be happy."

"And?"

"To make other people happy."

"And?"

Paris rolled her eyes. "You sound like a broken record."

"Maybe that's because you keep playing the same song, but you never get to the chorus. What do you *really* want?"

Admitting she needed anything other than being happy was hard. She'd spent most of her life hiding from the real Paris Haynes. She wore over-the-top clothes and tried to be the person everyone expected her to be. What she *really* wanted and who she was didn't matter. All that mattered was that she didn't end up like her mom.

"I'm waiting."

"I'm opening my flower shop in a few days. That's what I really want."

"What about outside of work? What kind of life do you want?"

Paris looked at the flowers on the workroom table. "You'll think it's silly."

"Nothing is ever silly."

With a glance at her friend, Paris picked up another flower. "I want to marry an incredible man, have three children, a dog, and a white picket fence."

Jackie sighed. "That sounds like bliss to me. Do you think Richard could fit into your plans?"

"He's happy with his life as it is."

"There's always room for improvement. Does he want more children?"

"I haven't asked."

"Maybe you should."

Paris grinned. "You don't just go up to someone you barely know and ask if they want more children."

"I can't see why not. If he says no, then you decide whether you want to spend more time with him."

"And what happens if he says yes?"

Jackie laughed. "I'll leave that up to you."

RICHARD OPENED the door to Blooming Lovely and looked around the store. Thankfully, Paris was busy helping a customer. All morning, he'd tried to decide whether coming here was a good idea. But it was Paris' last day, and he wanted her to know he was thinking about her.

Some of his nerves disappeared when she turned around. She was wearing a bright blue dress with yellow and pink flowers printed across the fabric. When she saw him, her smile made his decision to come here even more worthwhile.

After the customer left the store, she came to say hello. "I didn't expect to see you today. Have you finished work early?"

"I'm on my way to Anchor Lane. I thought I'd stop by and see how your last day's going."

"We've been busy since we opened, but I wouldn't have it any other way. It stops me from thinking about leaving."

"I know how that feels." Richard handed her the box he'd brought with him. "Normally, I would have brought you flowers to wish you luck, but that doesn't have the same impact when you're a florist."

"You didn't have to bring me anything."

Richard shrugged, hoping she didn't realize what a big deal it was to him.

Carefully, Paris unwrapped the box. When she saw what was inside, she smiled. "How did you know I have a sweet tooth?"

"You said you like the fudge from Sweet Treats, so I bought you a selection of flavors. If you're feeling a little stressed, the sugar might help."

"Thanks. It might come in handy sooner than you think."

"Why? What's happened?"

"Nadine's mom is changing a few wedding details. Their planner has called me three times to make sense of what she wants."

"The wedding's this weekend. Why is she making changes?"

Paris looked across the store at another customer. "I'm not sure Mrs. Kingston is ready for her daughter to get married."

"Do you think she's deliberately sabotaging their plans?"

"Not deliberately, but she's creating a lot of stress."

"Do you need me to do anything?"

Paris shook her head. "I'll be okay. I'm going to The Flower Cottage after work to create some more displays. Once they're done, I can focus on Nadine's wedding."

"If there's anything you need, I'm only a phone call away."

"Thanks. I'd better go. Mrs. Gilford looks as though she needs some help choosing her flowers." Paris kissed his cheek. "I appreciate you coming to see me." Slipping the fudge into her pocket, she hurried across the store.

Richard left Blooming Lovely with a smile on his face. It wasn't until he was almost at Anchor Lane that he realized how much difference Paris had made in his life.

Since he'd started working on her store, he hadn't stopped smiling. Except for the times when Tommy and the rest of the crew did something crazy.

He just hoped today wasn't one of those days.

Paris' heart pounded when someone tapped on the front door of The Flower Cottage. It was all very well working late, but when she was in a building with no one around her, every little squeak made her jump.

When she saw who was standing under the security light, she smiled. "This is a nice surprise."

Jack showed her his tool belt. "Dad said you're working. We brought our tools in case you need us to build something."

"I don't need anything built, but you could help me make some displays."

"What kind of displays?"

Richard handed Paris a large basket. "The kind that makes people want to hire Paris as their florist. I didn't know if you've had time for dinner, so I brought something for all of us."

As soon she lifted the lid, her stomach rumbled. "I haven't eaten anything since lunch, so this is lovely." Three containers of pasta and a delicious apple pie filled the basket. "I didn't know you were such a good cook."

"The hospitality class at Pastor John's church had some

leftovers. We put it with some things we got from the supermarket."

She smiled at Richard. "I thought you'd spent all evening cooking."

"Not tonight. Would you like to eat now or later?"

"Now would be great. We can sit in the kitchen. It's a lot tidier than in here."

On his way across the room, Jack looked at a large crystal chandelier hanging from the ceiling. "It's so sparkly."

Paris picked up some empty boxes, hoping it made everything look a little tidier. "It came from an old theater in Polson. It's my favorite thing in the entire room."

Jack stood in front of one of the displays she'd made. "I like this, too. Why is there a fire engine in the middle of the flowers?"

"It's to show people what I can do. Last year, I made some special flower arrangements for a dinner for the chief of the Polson Fire Department." Paris showed Jack a picture of the fire chief standing in front of his station. "This is Chief Morgan. He's been a firefighter for more than thirty years."

"That's a long time."

"It is. I used red flowers like these ones for the table decorations and made lots of goodie bags filled with candy-shaped fire engines. For this display, I've used dried flowers instead of fresh ones. Are you ready to see what your dad's doing in the kitchen?"

Jack nodded but didn't move. "Dad said you're probably too busy, but I've never had someone come to the mothers' and friends' day with me. Can you come with me? It's tomorrow."

She looked into Jack's wary gaze and her heart squeezed tight. Life could be tough when you're eight years old, especially when you're worried you don't fit in. "The parents' and friends' days aren't fun, are they?"

Jack frowned. "Did you have them at your school?"

"We had daddy and daughter days. My dad never came because he didn't live with me. I used to tell my mom I had a tummy ache whenever he was supposed to come to school."

"Where was your dad?"

"I don't know. He left one day and never came back."

"My mom left, too. Grandma and Granddad looked after me when I was little."

"You were lucky you had them." Paris pulled an old crate closer and sat down. "What would I have to do at the mothers' and friends' day?"

"My teacher said there will be running races, ten-pin bowling, and all kinds of things to try. You get points for doing stuff and extra ones if you win."

"And we'd do the activities together?"

Jack nodded. "If you don't want to do something, that's okay."

"What time does it start?"

"Ten o'clock. My teacher said we'll be finished by lunchtime."

She had so much to do. Spending two hours with Jack would make a huge difference in how prepared she was for Saturday. But she couldn't say no, not when he was looking at her like she was his last hope. Maybe if she started work early over the next couple of days, she could make up for the lost time.

"It's okay if you can't come."

Placing her hand on top of Jack's, she gave his fingers a gentle squeeze. "I'll be there, but I'm not a fast runner." His instant smile made her glad she'd said yes.

"It doesn't matter. Charlie said his mom can't run fast, either."

Paris smiled. Andrea would be thrilled to know what her

sons thought of her running abilities. "I'll be in good company, then."

Richard cleared his throat from beside the kitchen doorway. "Dinner's ready."

As soon as she looked at his face, she knew he'd heard at least some of what they'd said. "Jack's invited me to his school for the mothers' and friends' day."

"And Paris said yes," Jack added excitedly. "Except she can't run fast, but that's okay."

Richard looked at Paris, and her heart melted.

"Thank you," he said softly. "I know how much it means to Jack."

His words settled around her like a warm cocoon. "I'm looking forward to it. I might not be good at running, but I really enjoy ten-pin bowling."

Jack grinned. "Pastor John has a bowling competition at The Welcome Center. You should come with Dad and me."

"I didn't know there was bowling."

"Do you know about the movie nights?"

Paris shook her head. "It sounds like I need to spend less time at work."

"The Welcome Center has lots of good things happening. You could come with us. Dad won't mind."

Richard ruffled Jack's hair. "I definitely wouldn't mind, but Paris is hungry. You can tell her about all the activities while we're eating."

"Okay."

As Jack hurried into the kitchen, Richard turned to her. "You've made Jack's day. Are you sure you can go to school with him?"

"I'll make the time. It's important."

"What about your store and the wedding?"

"Kylie and Jackie are helping me get everything ready. I'll be okay."

Richard held her hand. "I'll bring dinner for everyone tomorrow night."

Paris knew she should tell him they'd be all right, but the warmth of his hand was short-circuiting her brain.

"Why didn't we get to know each other before now?" Richard asked.

"I don't know. Maybe we were too busy to make room for someone else in our lives."

"Or too worried about what the other person would say."

Her hand tightened around Richard's. "I'm not good at relationships, but I'd like to—"

"Dinner's ready!" Jack yelled from the kitchen.

Richard ran his fingertip down the side of her face. "What would you like to do?"

Paris' stomach churned. This was it. This was when she should tell him she wanted to be more than friends, that she enjoyed spending time with him and Jack, and that she wanted to spend even more time with them.

But her mom's voice rang in her head, telling her it would end in disaster. All she had to do was count the number of times her heart had been broken to know she was heading in the same direction.

"Paris?"

"I'd like to be your friend." The whispered words were so far from the truth that it hurt to say them.

Disappointment stole all the joy from Richard's face. "I'd like to be your friend, too. Let's get something to eat."

Paris walked into the kitchen and tried to pretend everything was okay. But it wasn't and, until she stopped listening to her mom's voice telling her she wasn't good enough, it never would be.

CHAPTER 13

*R*ichard sat in a black plastic chair opposite Peter
Bennett, the Chief Executive of BioTech Industries. His company had invented the neural gel prosthetic
attached to Richard's right leg. Each month, as part of the
clinical trial process, they met to discuss the effectiveness of
the prosthetic. So far, everything had gone better than
anyone expected.

"On a scale of one to ten, how would you rate the respon-
siveness of the prosthetic after the last software upgrade?"
Peter asked.

"Nine."

"Why not ten?"

Richard frowned. "You aren't supposed to question my
responses."

Peter smiled. "I'm the boss, and I'm curious."

He was also one of the nicest guys Richard had met. If it
weren't for Peter agreeing to add him to the trial group at the
last minute, he never would have been given the life-
changing prosthetic.

"I didn't give you a ten because it took three tries to

download the software."

"Everyone in Sapphire Bay was having issues with the Internet when you were doing the upgrade."

"It made a difference to my user experience."

Peter looked over the rim of his glasses. "Your expectations have increased since the trial started."

"So would yours if it was your leg we were assessing."

"Point taken. How can we improve on your score?"

"Better Internet?"

"I'm working on it. Is there anything else you want to discuss?"

Usually, Richard didn't have anything to add after the assessment was finished, but today was different. "I'm hoping you can give me some advice."

Peter closed his laptop and gave him his full attention. "I'll try."

He could have asked Ethan, his friend and the town's family therapist, about what was worrying him. Or he could have asked Pastor John. But, sometimes, he preferred not to dig too deeply into how he felt with his friends.

"This phase has the largest number of amputees. Has anyone mentioned how different wearing the neural gel prosthetics makes them feel?"

"In what way?"

Peter might think he was worrying about nothing, but having his leg blown off had left deep scars that had nothing to do with skin and bone. "In a new relationship kind of way. When I'm wearing the prosthetic, I look and move like everyone else. At some point, I'll have to show someone my stump. How have other people handled that?"

"I wish I had an easy answer for you, but I don't. I'm not a counselor, but what I do know is that everyone's different. It takes a lot of time and trust for some amputees to show people their stump. For others, they're upfront about their injury."

"What reactions do they get?" A sinking feeling hit Richard's stomach when Peter frowned. "Is it that bad?"

"Not necessarily. No matter how hard you want a relationship to work, nothing is ever guaranteed. It gets even more complicated when you have an injury that impacts your life. Are you sure you want to talk about this with me? Ethan's spoken to more amputees about relationship issues than I have."

"He's also my friend. If I tell him I'm worried about a woman seeing my stump, he'll think I have someone in mind."

"And you don't want to tell him who that person is?"

Richard looked through the window of Peter's office. "Sapphire Bay is a small town. I don't want her to be uncomfortable or feel sorry for me."

"Do you trust her?"

There was a gentleness and a fragility to Paris that he'd never taken the time to see. She treated everyone with kindness and respect, and wanted to make the world a better place. How could he not trust someone like that?

"I trust her."

"Do you want to show her your stump?"

"Definitely not, but I'd prefer to show her before our friendship goes any further. If she can't handle my stump and everything that goes with it, she isn't the person for me."

Peter nodded. "That makes sense."

"But?"

"You're more than what happened in Afghanistan. If she doesn't see anything other than friendship in your future, it doesn't matter."

That was easy for Peter to say. Richard's career in the

Army had shaped him into the person he was today. And some of it wasn't good.

"Talk to Ethan," Peter suggested. "He'll tell you something that will be more inspiring than what I've said."

Richard forced a smile. "He'll tell me there are more fish in the sea."

"He could be right, but it doesn't make up for the one you wanted to share your life with."

On that sobering thought, Richard picked up his jacket. "I need to collect Jack from his after-school program. Are we meeting here at the same time next month?"

"Unless I find a building for our research center, we will. If you need someone to talk to, you have my number."

"Thanks. Say hi to Katie from me." And before he spent more time thinking about the only fish in the sea he wanted to date, he left the room.

Peter might have developed state-of-the-art prosthetics, but it could never replace his actual leg. No matter how much he wished it could.

"READY. SET. GO!"

Paris tore across the grass toward the finish line. When she told Jack she'd come to the mothers' and friends' day, she didn't imagine she'd run anywhere. But Jack was more competitive than she thought. Adding another point to their tally was better than watching everyone else race. So, here she was, feet flying, arms pumping, and praying she didn't fall over.

She'd never been so glad to cross a finish line. By the time Jack joined her, she had her hands on her knees, gasping for breath.

"You did really good, Paris. You came fourth."

"Does that give us two points?"

Jack shook his head. "No. You had to come second or third for that."

"What's next?"

Jack consulted the crinkled piece of paper in his pocket. "The long jump. If our feet cross the painted line in front of the sandpit, we'll be disqualified."

Paris thought that was a little harsh considering this was a fun sports day, but some of the adults were sticklers for the rules. "I'll keep my foot away from the line."

"The sandpit's over here." As they made their way across the playground, Jack suddenly yelled, "Dad's here!"

Paris shielded her eyes from the sun and looked at where he was pointing.

Richard waved and Paris' traitorous heart gave a nervous flutter. Jack's dad might not be too concerned about her flamboyant dresses, but she wondered what he'd think of the matching T-shirts she'd bought for the day.

When Richard saw them, his eyebrows rose. "I didn't know you liked Legos, Paris."

"I'm not as big a fan as Jack, but I appreciate the skill that goes into building the models. I thought this design would give us the winning edge." Their matching T-shirts had black backgrounds with bright, fluorescent Legos blocks covering the front and back.

"We're called The Blockbusters," Jack said proudly. "Did you see Paris run? She's much faster than most of the other moms."

Richard placed his arm around Jack's shoulders. "I didn't see the race, but I'm glad Paris did well. What's next?"

"The long jump. We'd better hurry. Otherwise, Mrs. Smith might think we aren't coming."

Paris stuck her floppy straw hat on her head. "Lead the way, block master."

The gleam in Richard's eyes followed her the entire way across the playground.

While Jack let the teacher know they'd arrived, Paris waited with Richard. "It's great you could get some time off work. Jack's happy you're here."

"I was hoping to arrive sooner, but I had to sort out a problem. Are you enjoying yourself?"

"It's better than I thought. Jack's happy with how many points we've scored and I haven't fallen over. As an added bonus, everyone gets a bag of candy from Sweet Treats at the end of the competition.

Richard smiled. "You can't beat that. Do you need a hand with anything in the store tonight?"

"I should be okay. Kylie and Jackie are helping me."

"If you need more pairs of hands, Jack and I will be there, too."

"I'll keep it in mind."

Jack raced across to them. "We're number five, Paris. Everyone's lining up now."

She grinned at Richard. "We'll see you on the other side of the sandpit."

"I'll look forward to it."

As she followed Jack to the line of people waiting for their turn, she glanced back at Richard. How anyone could look so good in a pair of blue jeans and a sweatshirt was beyond her. But *he* could, and she wasn't the only person who'd noticed.

EARLY ON SATURDAY MORNING, Paris added the finishing touches to the bridal bouquet for Nadine. Made from pale pink peony roses and lush, green foliage, it was absolutely stunning. In an hour, Nadine's brother would collect the bridal party's flowers and, hopefully, take good care of them. Paris' biggest concern was keeping them fresh for the late afternoon wedding, but Nadine was confident they'd be okay.

Agreeing to provide the flowers for larger events was exciting, but Paris needed to plan her workflow differently. If it weren't for her friends, she'd be in serious trouble. Kylie and Jackie had helped create the table decorations on Thursday evening. And, on Friday, Mabel and Andrea had rolled up their sleeves and completed phase one of the design for the wedding arches.

Combined with the opening of The Flower Cottage, this weekend was a mammoth undertaking. Even without Nadine's mom's changes, she'd underestimated how much help she'd need.

Jackie opened the back door of The Flower Cottage. "Good morning. How does it feel to be opening your store today?"

Paris placed the bouquet in a box and sighed. "I've been too busy to worry about anything. Nadine's mom called me last night to ask if I could make another corsage. I just hope she doesn't have any more requests before her daughter gets married."

"If I were being uncharitable, I'd say she's taking advantage of you."

"She only wants Nadine and Carl's wedding to be perfect. How are you?"

Jackie grinned. "Happy to be here to celebrate the official opening of The Flower Cottage." With a flourish, she took a bottle of champagne from behind her back. "And we can't do that without a glass of bubbles."

"That sounds wonderful, but I haven't had breakfast. If I drink any alcohol, I'll be dancing on the counters."

"Not if you have some of these yummy treats." Andrea

walked into the workroom holding another box. "I had a feeling you'd be here super early, so I made everyone breakfast."

Paris smiled at her friends. "You guys are amazing. Thank you."

"That's what friends are for." The bacon and egg croissant Andrea handed to Paris smelled divine. "You should open your own café. This looks incredible."

Jackie handed everyone a glass of champagne. "I can guarantee it will taste even better. Let's make a toast. To Paris and her wonderful flower shop. May you have all the success you deserve and lots of customers who adore your arrangements."

Andrea smiled. "And some great publicity from the Kingston's wedding."

Paris clinked her glass against her friends'. "Thank you. I couldn't have done this without you."

"I'm glad we could help." Andrea bit into a croissant and smiled. "If I don't say so myself, this is delicious."

Paris suddenly remembered they were missing two little somebodies. "Where are the boys?" she asked Andrea.

"Katie organized a weekend writing retreat at The Welcome Center. They won't be home until Sunday morning."

"Your house must have been quiet this morning."

"That's one of the reasons I'm here so early." Andrea picked up her glass of champagne. "The house doesn't feel the same without them."

Paris hugged her. "Don't worry. They'll be back soon, and then you'll wish you had a few minutes to yourself."

"In the meantime," Jackie said with a grin, "let's enjoy breakfast and then help Paris. What do you still need to do?"

She picked up her clipboard. "I still have two garlands to make for the Kingston's wedding and a few posies for the shop. After that, all I need to do is get everything ready for a nine o'clock opening."

"I'll make the garlands," Andrea said. "Is it the same design as the ones we did yesterday?"

"It is."

Jackie wiped her hands on a napkin. "I'll make the posies and help open the store."

"Just you wait and see," Andrea said. "Today will be so much fun."

Paris didn't know if 'fun' was the word she'd use, but it was better than 'a disaster'. Especially when two hundred people were descending on Sapphire Bay for the wedding of the year.

RICHARD LOOKED over the heads of the people waiting to get into Paris' store. The Flower Cottage had only been open for an hour, and the line of customers was through the door and halfway to the general store.

While he was waiting outside, he'd only heard good things from the people who'd already been inside. They were blown away by her displays and the gifts they'd bought. If everyone continued to support her, she wouldn't have to worry about staying in business.

His gaze wandered along the eight cottages standing side-by-side on Anchor Lane. Remodeling Paris' store first was a wise decision. From the discussions going on around him, some of the people who'd come to the opening were interested in renting the other buildings. That would make Penny extremely happy.

He knew how much it cost to make the buildings functional and attractive. Without interest from prospective tenants, the county could decide to limit the funding they were providing.

"Richard? What are you doing standing in the line?"

He smiled at Jackie. "I'm waiting to see Paris' amazing store like everyone else. I thought you'd be at the Kingston's house by now."

"We're leaving in a few minutes. I told Paris I'd check how many people are still waiting to come inside."

Richard looked over her shoulder. "Lots."

"Well, there's one less now." Jackie grabbed his arm and led him inside. "I'm glad Paris asked a couple of the people from her adult flower decorating class to help. So far, she's sold out of all the local crafts we unpacked, and she has enough flower orders to keep her busy for the next month."

He couldn't have been happier for her. "I can't believe there are so many people here."

"That's small-town life for you. Everyone wants to help make The Flower Cottage a success."

Looking at the people here today, he had to agree with Jackie. In one corner of the room, the host of the local radio station was broadcasting live from The Flower Cottage. Mabel Allen, in her role as administrator of the community Facebook page, was taking photos of what was happening. And, if he wasn't mistaken, at least one reporter was preparing a story for the newspapers.

Paris stood behind the sales counter. Her dress was bright pink and covered in pictures of lollipops. As she listened intently to the customer, she nodded and made notes on her laptop. Hopefully, they were discussing an event she could decorate.

Jackie stopped in front of an empty set of shelves. "I'll let Paris know you're here."

"It's okay. I'll say hello once she's finished helping her customer."

"You'll have to interrupt. Otherwise, you could be waiting for a long time."

"I don't mind." Richard could watch Paris for hours. She had the type of personality that drew him to her, even from a distance. "Jack's playing at a friend's house. Do you want me to follow you to the Kingston's? I could help set up the big floral arrangements."

Jackie looked relieved. "That would be incredible. The large arrangements need to be hooked over the frames. Kylie keeps telling me she can attach them, but I don't want her anywhere near a ladder. Even if you can only spare an hour, it would be great."

"I'll stay as long as you need me."

"In that case, I'll see you at the Kingston's."

Richard nodded. "I won't be long." Paris looked as though she had everything under control. Everyone was enjoying themselves and spending lots of money. If he could make her day a little easier by helping at her first major event, he'd do it.

CHAPTER 14

*P*aris checked her watch. She'd started work at five o'clock this morning, and it didn't look like she'd be going home anytime soon. Nadine and Carl were dancing the night away, surrounded by their family and friends. Everyone was having a wonderful time.

Holding her hand over her mouth, she stifled a yawn.

"Long day?"

She sent Shelley a tired smile. "I had an early morning. John did a lovely service."

"He was a little nervous. It's not often you have a video production company from Los Angeles filming you."

"Or a world-famous photographer capturing the day."

Shelley laughed. "He's worried he'll be on the cover of tomorrow's newspaper."

"If he is, he'll look the part. His white robe looked stunning against the floral background."

"That's because Nadine and Carl had the best florist in Montana decorating their wedding. You must have bought a lot of flowers to do all the arrangements."

"Enough to fill a shipping container." Paris still couldn't

believe she'd managed to source and store so many flowers in such a short time. "I'm still in awe of what we've done. From the moment the guests stepped onto the Kingston's property, they've been surrounded by flowers."

"I'm glad it worked out." Shelley tilted her head to the side. "I saw Jackie and Kylie before the wedding. They said Richard was a great help."

Paris kept her gaze locked on the wedding guests. If Shelley thought she was interested in Richard, she'd do everything she could to get them together. "It was good of him to help. His extra height came in handy on the ladder."

"Why do you think he spent his Saturday helping Jackie and Kylie?"

"Because he saw how busy they were and wanted to help."

"He likes you, that's why."

"Richard likes a lot of people."

Shelley sighed. "Sometimes, you can be so stubborn."

"I'm not the only one. I thought you'd be too busy with what's happening in the church to worry about Richard and me."

"I'm never too busy to ignore my two favorite people. You're perfect together."

"I'm not good at relationships."

"You just haven't met the right person."

Paris wasn't ready to admit that Shelley could be right. She'd only had three boyfriends. Each time she dated someone, she had low expectations about where it could lead. And, if she was ever under an illusion that something was working, her mom was quick to tell her she was making a mistake.

She watched the bride and groom spin in a slow circle on the dance floor. Nadine's veil floated behind her, giving the photographer the perfect shot.

Paris frowned. "How do you know if someone is the right person for you?"

Instead of the wise reply she was expecting, Shelley laughed. "I'm the worst person to ask. John drove me crazy for the first few weeks I knew him. I would have bet everything I owned that we'd never end up together."

"What changed?"

"He told me about his life, what he'd seen and done, and why he wanted to work in Sapphire Bay. It helped me see the real John McDonald. Now, I can't imagine my life without him." Shelley nodded toward the wedding guests. "Nadine and Carl are getting ready to leave."

Paris looked across the dance floor. The bridesmaids were standing in a line opposite the groomsmen. Their bouquets formed an arch that Nadine and Carl were about to run under. As if on cue, the photographer and videographer stood at one end, capturing the happy moment.

A knot of sadness lodged in Paris' throat. It took courage to tell someone you loved them, and determination to make the relationship last. Until now, she hadn't had either. She'd spent most of her life with people who weren't looking for happy ever after.

Knowing there was someone in the world who would always be there for you, someone who would help you be the best version of yourself, was as foreign to her as flying to the moon.

Since she'd moved to Sapphire Bay, she found peace, true friends, and a man who could teach her how to fly. All she had to do was tell him how she felt. And that would be harder than moving halfway across the country and starting her own business.

❄

Richard knocked on Paris' front door and waited. He just hoped she was awake and not having a relaxing morning in bed.

"Do you think she's home, Dad?" Jack asked.

"I'm not sure. I'll knock again in case she's down the other end of the house." After church this morning, Jack had asked John and Shelley if he could take Toto for a walk. The adorably scruffy puppy was sitting beside him, like the most well-behaved dog in the world.

That lasted for all of ten seconds. As soon as Toto heard the front door opening, he jumped up and bounded toward Paris. Thankfully, Jack was holding the leash firmly and saved Paris from the excited fur ball coming toward her.

Her instant smile was good to see. "This is a wonderful surprise." She kneeled on the veranda and patted Toto. "How was the writing retreat, Jack?"

"It was fun. I finished my story, and Katie's going to show us how to publish our books."

"That's fantastic."

"Pastor John said we could take Toto for a walk, so I asked Dad if we could come and see you. Were you having a sleep-in?"

Paris shook her head. "I wish I was. I've been catching up on my housework."

"I don't like doing chores. Do you want to come for a walk with us?"

Her eyes lifted to Richard's. His heart pounded and everything around him stilled. Even in a blue tracksuit, Paris was beautiful. "We'd enjoy your company."

"I'd love to, but I need to collect some flowers from the Kingston's house at eleven-thirty."

Richard frowned. "Do you normally do that?"

"No. Nadine's parents are donating some of the arrangements to another couple getting married this afternoon. I said I'd pick them up."

"Do you want us to give you a hand?"

"Not today. John organized some volunteers to help. As soon we've packed the flowers into their trucks, they'll take them straight to the church." Toto wriggled closer to her legs. Paris stroked his back and smiled. "How can I resist such a cutie? The vacuuming can wait for another day. As long as I'm back here in an hour, I'll have enough time to drive to the Kingston's."

Jack grinned. "You can hold Toto's leash if you want to."

"I'd like that. I'll just grab my jacket."

While she was getting ready, Richard looked around the front yard. The garden was as colorful as Paris. Daisies, roses, and wildflowers surrounded the house and ran along the front fence. Red bricks placed in a herringbone pattern formed a walkway to the veranda, welcoming visitors to the cottage.

"I'm ready."

Richard's eyebrows rose. "You're a 49ers fan?"

Paris pulled up the zipper on her football jacket. "I'm a fan of anything from San Francisco. I lived there for three years and loved every minute."

"Will you ever go back?"

"Not to live, but I'd like to visit my friends."

He breathed a sigh of relief. It hadn't crossed his mind that she'd leave Sapphire Bay, especially after opening her own business.

Jack pulled Toto away from the mailbox. "I was only little when we came to Sapphire Bay. Grandma and Granddad are the only people I remember from before we lived here."

"Grandparents are the best kind of people to remember," Paris assured him.

Jack nodded and raced ahead with Toto.

"Have you visited the animal shelter yet?" Paris asked Richard.

"We're going there next week. I have a feeling Jack won't want to adopt a kitten after spending time with Toto."

"That's because he's cute."

"So is someone else I know."

A blush warmed Paris' cheeks. "Are you flirting with me?"

"I'm trying," he mumbled. "But I'm a little rusty."

"You're doing great."

Richard frowned. "You don't mind?"

She shook her head. "But I have to tell you a secret. I'm a little rusty, too."

"You don't seem rusty to me."

"Looks can be deceptive."

Paris seemed so sad he wondered what she was thinking. "Does it have anything to do with the stickability issue you told me about?"

"You have a good memory."

He held out his hand. "Why do you think you have a problem committing to anything?" When Paris' fingers wrapped around his, a weight lifted from his shoulders.

"I've only had a few boyfriends, but each relationship ended faster than I could blink. I was so busy trying to find the perfect life, that I wasn't happy with anything."

"Is that why you left San Francisco?"

Paris shook her head. "I'd already realized a perfect life doesn't exist. I left because my boyfriend was sleeping with someone I trusted. I needed to do something drastic to stop repeating the same mistakes I'd made."

"Why did you decide to live in Sapphire Bay?"

"I'm usually organized, but moving here was one of the most random things I've ever done. I found a map of America, closed my eyes, and drove to the nearest town my finger landed on."

He laughed. "That wasn't much different from what I did. I heard about John's support group from a friend. Other than that, I knew nothing about Sapphire Bay."

"And look at us now," she said with a smile. "We have our own businesses, our own homes, and have made some wonderful friends."

Richard held her hand a little tighter. "And we've met each other."

"What about stickability?"

"As long as we're honest with each other, we won't have to worry about stickability."

Paris sighed and looked across at Jack. "That sounds good to me. Apart from Jack, what else is important to you?"

"My family, friends, and having a good life. What about you?"

"The only family I have is my mom, and we don't have a great relationship."

"What happened?"

She looked down at her sneakers. "Mom is an alcoholic. Most of the time, you wouldn't know she's been drinking. It's only when things aren't going well that she crumbles. She has high expectations about what I should do with my life, and I'm always disappointing her."

"That must be stressful."

"It is." Paris took a deep breath. "I used to think that when I was an adult, everything would be better. But it got worse. Growing up with someone telling you you're not good enough broke something inside of me. The only way I can focus on building a great life is to spend as little time with her as possible."

"How does she feel about that?"

"She would be happier if I lived in Los Angeles. The only good thing about her job is that it keeps her busy. What happened to Jack's mom?"

Richard watched Jack throw a stick into the air. "I met Angie when we were at college. I joined the army, we got married, had Jack, and then I left for Afghanistan. She was on her own with a new baby, and it became too much. Mom and Dad tried to help her, but she wanted to do everything herself. The day after she was told about my injury, she left Jack with my parents and moved to Vancouver. She died a year later from a drug overdose."

"I'm sorry."

"It was an awful time. No one knows why she was taking the pain medication she was on, but she took too much. Throughout everything, my parents were incredible."

Jack ran toward them. "Look what I found." He held two flat stones in the palm of his hand.

Toto looked up at Richard, then at Jack. It was almost as if he realized what was coming next.

"How many times do you think they'll skip across the water?"

He held one of the stones in the air and gave it to Richard. "This one will do five skips. And *this* one will do six."

His smile made Richard laugh. "I'll bet a double scoop of vanilla ice cream that this stone will skip seven times across the water."

"Deal!" Jack yelled as he raced toward the water.

Paris laughed. "Why do I get the feeling you've spent a lot of time skipping stones?"

"We come here at least twice a week. This is the first time I've said I'll skip a stone seven times."

"Two scoops of ice cream is a good incentive."

A warmth spread through his chest. He enjoyed seeing Paris happy, knowing he'd helped ease the heartache of her life with her mother. "You have a point, especially when it's vanilla. Do you want to have a go?"

"You might regret asking me."

"Are you good?"

She leaned forward and kissed his cheek. "I'm better than good. I'm amazing. If I find the right stone, I'll make it skip eight times for a chocolate-dipped ice cream."

He looked into her eyes and wondered why it had taken so long for them to become friends. "And if you can't beat Jack and me?"

"I'll buy everyone whatever dessert they want."

"That's a big promise."

"Skipping stones is a serious business."

Richard smiled and led her to the shore. "The best stones are usually closest to the water."

Paris scanned the ground before showing him a stone. "Like this one?"

The flat stone said a lot about Paris' skipping stone experience. "You weren't kidding when you said you're good."

"Amazing," Paris corrected. "I used to do this all the time with my granddad."

Jack hurried toward them with Toto yapping at his heels. "Are you ready?"

Richard nodded. For the first time in years, he was ready for anything life threw at him. Including a woman who would give him any dessert he wanted, as long as his skipping stone didn't let him down.

CHAPTER 15

*O*n Wednesday, Richard carried the chocolate cake he'd made to the church's main meeting room. Shelley, John's wife, had offered to bake a birthday cake for Jack, but Richard wanted to make it himself. He'd searched the Internet, finally finding a cake that came highly recommended, and hoped for the best.

He couldn't believe Jack was nine years old today. It only seemed like yesterday he'd brought him home from the hospital with Angie. They'd been excited about the future and scared of looking after a newborn baby. Today, thinking about the time he'd spent with his family before going to Afghanistan made him sad.

No one knew whether Angie's overdose was a mistake or intentional but, either way, it didn't matter. Jack had lost his mom, and Richard had lost his best friend.

Jack raced toward him. "Pastor John forgot the ketchup. He's going back to the church to get it."

"That's good. When we're outside the meeting room, can you open the door? I don't want to drop the cake."

Jack kept pace with him. "Nora said you must be clever to bake a cake."

Nora was Jack's friend. They spent a lot of time together at the after school-programs. "I'm not sure about clever, but I'm pleased with how it turned out. What do you think?"

Jack's gaze moved to the whale-shaped cake. "It's the best birthday cake ever."

A warmth spread through Richard's chest. He'd stressed about decorating it, worried it wouldn't turn out as good as the picture he'd seen. Creating the pale gray frosting had been a mission but, once the blue waves covered the worst bits, it looked pretty good.

He held the box a little tighter. "After the cake is on the table, all we need to do is hang the banners."

"When will everyone arrive?"

"Soon. We told them to be here at four o'clock, and it's nearly that now."

Wednesday afternoons were usually quiet in the village, but not today. Jack had wanted to invite everyone to his birthday, which was why they were having it in the church. Instead of presents, they'd asked everyone to bring a small plate of food to share.

When he walked into the meeting room, Richard was surprised at how much decorating had been done. In the time it took him to go home and collect the cake, the banners had been strung across the windows, and helium-filled balloons bobbed against the ceiling.

"What do you think?" John asked from behind him.

"It's fantastic."

"It's amazing," Jack said in awe. "Look at all the food."

Richard's eyes widened when he saw the table. There wasn't a spare inch of space for another plate. "Where did it come from?"

Before John could reply, the main doors burst open. Jack's friends streamed into the room, singing "Happy Birthday".

Richard placed the cake on a small table and lit the candles. Instead of being overwhelmed with all the attention, Jack was enjoying every moment.

After the candles had been blown out, Jack thanked his friends for coming. As music filled the room, everyone started talking, eating, and enjoying each other's company.

Shelley stood beside Richard. "It's a lovely party. You did a great job of the cake."

"Thanks. It wasn't as easy as I thought it would be."

"They never are. Jack's enjoying himself."

Richard smiled. Jack was dancing under a large disco ball with Nora, Charlie, and Andy. "It's good to have something to celebrate."

"You can say that again. The last few months have been hectic. You must be getting ready to move into your new home?"

"I pick up the keys on Friday." Paris walked into the room. She was wearing one of her 1950s floral dresses—the kind with bright pink petticoats and matching sneakers.

"Someone else is having a busy week." Shelley touched his arm. "Go and say hello. While you're doing that, I'll congratulate the birthday boy."

Why did he get the feeling Shelley was turning into his fairy godmother? Whether or not she had a magic wand hidden in her office, he wasn't wasting any time. Before anyone else could talk to Paris, he hurried across the room.

"Hi, Richard. I'm sorry I wasn't here to see Jack blow out the candles on his cake. I was held up at work."

"It's okay. Mabel videoed the whole thing. I'll send you a copy."

"That would be great. How does it feel to have a nine-year-old living with you?"

"I'm not sure." He had so many conflicting emotions inside of him. He didn't know if he could explain how he felt, even to himself. "I'm proud of the person Jack's turning into, but I'm worried about the choices he'll make as he gets older. I can't be there all the time to make sure he's okay."

Paris' hand slipped into his. "Most parents probably feel the same way. You love him, and that's all that matters."

"And we've all made mistakes."

"Some more than others." Paris smiled. "What else have you planned for today?"

Gently, he pushed a strand of hair over Paris' ear. "We're hoping a busy florist might join us at the lake for a picnic dinner."

"I'd like that, especially if we have another skipping stone competition."

Richard smiled. "It will be impossible to beat the seven skips you did last time."

"Nice try, but it was eight."

"Are you sure?"

"Positive. This time, Jack can decide what the winner gets."

Richard knew exactly what his son would want. "He'd like that, although it might mean a trip to the animal shelter."

"That's okay. They have lots of cats at the moment."

Before he could ask how she knew about the cats, Jack raced toward them.

"Dad! Look what Katie gave me." He held a book in his hand. "It's my story, the one I wrote in the writing class."

Richard's eyes widened. The paperback looked like any other novel you'd find in a bookstore. "It looks fantastic."

"I drew the cover," Jack told Paris. "Dad helped me find some pictures of space rockets on the Internet. We made up the rest."

"You did a great job. Did you know Katie was giving you the book today?"

Jack shook his head. "She said it's a birthday surprise. She hasn't made any of the other books yet."

"You're really lucky."

Richard looked inside the book. The pictures they'd drawn for the beginning of each chapter looked great. And, at the end of the story, Katie had included a picture of Jack holding Mr. Snuggles. "We'll have to ask Katie if we can buy more copies. Grandma would love one."

"So would I," Paris said. "I'll tell everyone I know a wonderful author."

Jack beamed with pleasure. "I'll find Katie. She said she can print as many copies as we need. Next week, we're uploading all the stories onto Amazon."

After he'd left, Paris leaned against Richard's arm. "Jack is an amazing boy. He makes me happier just being around him."

"He's an amazing and *excited* boy. We might need to go for a long walk after dinner to burn off some of his energy."

"That sounds like the perfect end to a perfect day," Paris said softly.

Richard agreed. Especially when they'd be spending their evening together.

PARIS BOWED FROM HER WAIST, accepting Jack's applause like a seasoned professional.

"Are you sure you don't have a secret weapon hidden up the sleeves of your T-shirt?" Richard asked.

"Remember to be a good sport. I beat you fair and square."

"Paris could make a stone skip twelve times if she wanted," Jack said happily.

"I'm not sure about twelve," she told him. "I'm happy with seven, especially when your dad only managed four."

Richard closed the lid on the picnic basket. "It might have only been four skips, but they were a solid four. Where are we going next?"

"To the animal shelter." Jack rolled up the blanket and held it close. "It's open late tonight."

Paris smiled. She didn't like Richard's chances of leaving the shelter without a pet.

"I've been looking on the animal shelter's website," Jack said as they walked toward Richard's truck. "They have a lot of animals at the moment."

Richard lifted the picnic basket into the back of the truck. "We don't have to choose a pet today. We can go back next week to have another look."

"It's okay. I'm a good looker."

And that, Paris thought, was that. Tonight, whether Richard was ready or not, he would become the proud father of his first fur baby in Sapphire Bay.

JACK'S NOSE twitched as he opened the door to the cat room. "It's smelly in here."

"It's the kitty litter." Richard looked around the room. Four cats were sitting inside a climbing frame, and another two were asleep on the back of an old sofa. They all looked well-fed, content, and not very mischievous—the perfect pet to take to their new home.

Jack looked at one of the posters on the wall, and then patted a ginger cat. "This is Marmalade. She's five years old."

Paris patted another cat. She smiled when both cats started purring. "They're happy to see us."

"Not as happy as the kittens," Jack said. "They jumped all over me."

The thought of having a hyperactive kitten in the house made Richard nervous. If it escaped, he'd never catch it if he wasn't wearing his prosthetic. "They were really cute, but they won't be kittens forever. Before you know it, they'll be as big as Marmalade."

"But it won't be for ages," Jack said quickly.

Paris tickled a black cat under his chin. "They love being cuddled."

"I know, but they aren't the same as a kitten."

Jack sounded so disappointed that Richard felt terrible for wanting to adopt an older cat.

"Why don't we visit the kennels?" Paris suggested.

Richard sent Paris a grateful glance.

"Dad doesn't want me to have a dog."

"You don't have to adopt one," Paris said gently. "It would be nice to say hello to them. They might not get as many visitors as the kittens and cats."

Jack looked up at Richard.

He held out his hand. "I'm happy to visit the dogs if you are?"

Jack's small hand settled in Richard's. "I don't know how many dogs are in the shelter."

"It will be fun finding out."

"I suppose so."

Paris opened the door. "I saw some pictures of the dogs on Facebook the other day. There's a sweet Chihuahua called Charlie. We could ask if you could hold him."

"Do you think that would be okay?"

Richard shrugged. "I can't see why not." Before Jack decided he'd sooner go back to the kittens, they followed the signs to the kennels. It didn't take long for them to find Charlie.

Jack kneeled in front of his pen. "He's so small."

Charlie's tail wagged energetically.

"I think he likes you," Paris whispered.

Within a few minutes, Jack was holding Charlie and asking a staff member all sorts of questions about dogs. When they were invited on a tour of the kennels, Jack said yes straightaway.

Richard wasn't worried about visiting the kennels. The puppies were in another area, so that reduced the chance of Jack falling in love with one. As they moved from pen to pen, the staff member told them how they look after the dogs, how they train them, and what they do to find their forever homes.

While Jack and Paris patted a Cocker Spaniel, Richard walked farther down the aisle. Although the dogs seemed happy, it wasn't the same as living with a family who cared about you.

When he reached the last pen, he looked at a dog with the saddest eyes he'd ever seen. With his shaggy, brown coat and pointy ears, he could have been a cross between three or four different breeds.

"That's Louie," another staff member said. "He's been with us for six months."

"That's a long time to keep a rescue dog."

"It is, but Louie's special. He was brought to the shelter after someone ran over him with their truck. The poor guy's had so many surgeries that it's hard to remember a time when he wasn't on pain medication."

"Has anyone wanted to give him a home?"

"Not yet. He's a high-needs dog. The chance of finding anyone to look after him isn't great. It's a real shame because he's a super sweet dog."

Richard held out his hand. Louie sniffed but didn't come closer.

"He's wary of strangers. He must have had a hard life before he came here."

Jack hurried down the aisle. "I found a dog that looks like Mr. Snuggles. Come and see him."

Richard took a last look at Louie before turning to Jack. He hoped someone gave him a good home before it was too late.

Jack started to say something, then stopped. As he stared at the pen, his smile disappeared and tears filled his eyes.

"What's wrong?" Richard turned around to look at what had upset him.

Louie was hopping toward the gate. His eyes never left Richard's as he tried hard to get closer to them on his three legs.

"We had to amputate his back leg when he arrived," the staff member explained. "It was too damaged to save."

Richard's heart pounded as he moved closer to Louie. Tears stung his eyes when he realized why he looked so sad. It was almost as if the little guy realized they shared the same challenges, the same grief that never disappeared.

"He likes you, Dad."

Bending down, he held his hand against the wire fence. Louie sniffed and then sighed.

"I haven't seen him do that before," the staff member said. "Would you like me to open the pen?"

Richard nodded and Jack sat beside him on the concrete floor.

"You have to talk real quiet in case he's scared," Jack whispered. "What's his name?"

"Louie. He's been here a long time." Richard lowered himself to the floor and waited to see what would happen.

Cautiously, Louie hopped toward them. When Richard

reached out to pat him, Louie leaned into his hand. Even though his coat was uneven, his fur was soft and silky. If he were a cat, he'd be purring by now.

Paris joined them. "Have you found a friend?"

"His name is Louie," Jack said. "One of his legs is missing, just like Dad's."

Paris' gaze connected with Richard's. The probability of them finding a dog with an amputated limb was about as high as Louie being adopted, and she knew it.

"What are you going to do?" she asked.

"Could we take him home, Dad?"

"If he wants to come with us, we could."

Jack hugged Louie. "What do you think, boy? Do you want to live with us?"

Louie's pink tongue licked the side of Jack's face, making him laugh.

After that, there was only one thing Richard could do.

Louie had just found his forever home.

CHAPTER 16

The following day, Paris was closing The Flower Cottage when Andrea walked into the store. "This is a nice surprise. How are you?"

"I'm doing better now that I'm here. I've been trying to get away from Mabel, but she wanted to talk about the Christmas events she's organizing."

"She's starting early."

"You know Mabel. She wants everything to be perfect. But that's not why I'm here." Andrea took a deep breath. "I want to ask your advice about something."

Paris turned the sign on the door to "Closed" and smiled at her friend. "Now we can talk without being interrupted. Tell me what's on your mind."

"Each time I visit your store, there are lots of people walking down Anchor Lane. They want to see your flowers and look at what's happening to the cottages. Once all the stores are open, Anchor Lane will become even more popular."

"Richard's construction crew is doing an amazing job. All

Penny has to do is find—" Paris' eyes widened. "Are you thinking of leasing one of the cottages?"

Andrea nodded. "I know it's crazy, but I want to open a café. I worked in the hospitality industry before I had the boys, and I loved every minute. But I have no idea how to run my own business. I don't even know if people will like my food."

"You'd be fantastic. You bake the yummiest food and this location would be perfect for a café. You wouldn't believe the number of customers who want to sit somewhere and enjoy a good cup of coffee."

"Sweet Treats is the closest café to Anchor Lane. I hope Megan and Brooke will be okay with what I want to do."

"Brooke only started selling coffee because there weren't many options in town. I don't think she'll mind if you open a café."

Andrea sighed. "That's good, but there's another problem. I don't have a lot of money to invest in the store. What kind of expenses did you have?"

Paris walked across to the front counter and opened her laptop. "I'll print you a copy of my business case. The layout changes I needed were covered by Penny. It didn't add a lot of extra cost because the construction crew hadn't been working on the cottage for very long. I found the shelving and furniture on eBay. The only things I had to buy locally were the materials for the displays, the flowers, and the boxes and paper I use. Which cottage are you thinking of leasing?"

"The one beside yours. The small strip of lawn in the front of the building would be perfect for a few tables and chairs. I could hang baskets of flowers under the veranda and string fairy lights around the trim."

"That would be lovely. Have you been inside the cottage?"

Andrea shook her head. "Not yet. I wanted to see if you thought it was a good idea before I do anything else."

"Well, you've come at the right time. Do you want to go exploring now?"

"I'd love to, but I don't have a key."

Paris opened a drawer. "This one will work. Richard changed all the locks, so they're the same as my cottage. If the construction crew can't get inside, they ask me for this key."

"That makes sense. Do you think Penny will mind?"

"We'll know if a few seconds." Paris took out her phone and called her friend. After she'd finished speaking, she found the hardhats Richard had left in her store. "As long as we wear these and sign the safety register, we can have a look."

Andrea grinned. "If I open the café, I won't have far to go if I don't know how to do something."

"And I'll know where to go for a hot chocolate and a delicious muffin." Paris shut the door behind them. "Keep an open mind when you see the cottage. I'm not sure what the construction crew has done."

"As long as it has running water and electricity, it has potential."

Paris couldn't guarantee either of those things, but Andrea had a good imagination. If anyone could make an old cottage into a gorgeous café, it was her.

THE FIRST THING Paris saw when she opened the door was the kitchen. The original wooden cabinets were still there, along with an orange Formica counter that looked like it belonged in the 1970s. "This is worse than the kitchen that was in my cottage."

"It's not too bad." Andrea opened a cupboard and peered inside. "I'd have to replace everything with commercial grade appliances and surfaces, but some of the cupboards could be reused."

"Is the kitchen big enough?"

"I think so." She held out her arms and stood in front of a wall. "I'd put an oven here. If I buy an upright, multi-level model, it won't take as much room as a conventional oven. Two microwaves could go here." She moved to the next wall. "Refrigerators and freezers here, and the sink and commercial dishwasher could go under the window."

"That won't give you much counter space."

"It will if we move the wall out a couple of feet. That would give me enough room for a stainless steel, free-standing counter in the center of the room. I'd take the doors off the cupboards and make them into open shelves. It will look amazing, but it will be expensive."

"Can you buy second-hand appliances?"

"I'd have to." Andrea turned on a power switch and two fluorescent bulbs sprung to life. "That's a good sign."

They wandered into the next room.

"I was hoping it would be the same as your cottage, and it is." Andrea smiled at the brick fireplace nestled against one wall. "It's perfect. Even with extending the kitchen, there's plenty of room for the tables and chairs. If I removed the walls on either side of the hallway, it would open up the entire front of the cottage."

"It would look gorgeous."

Andrea stared at the same pressed tin ceiling that was in Paris' cottage. "The only issue I have is the cost."

"Why don't you speak to Brooke? She would have gone through the same thing before she opened Sweet Treats."

"Good idea. And if I do some of the work myself, it might make it less expensive."

Paris frowned. The Flower Cottage had cost more than she thought, but she didn't have to install a commercial kitchen on top of the other expenses. "Why do you want to open a café?"

"My mom was a great cook. From when I was little, she showed me how to bake delicious cookies and cakes. When I was older, we made recipes from around the world. Baking makes me happy and, when other people enjoy my food, it makes me even happier."

"Before I opened The Flower Cottage, Richard warned me that owning a business takes more time than you realize. Would Charlie and Andy be okay if you're working more hours?"

"I want them to see that having a dream and working hard toward it are important. If that means spending a little less time together for a while, then it's worth it. Mr. Jessop said he'd look after the boys when I'm working, so it's a win-win situation for everyone."

Mr. Jessop was the gardener at The Welcome Center and an honorary granddad to Andrea's two boys. They'd lived together for more than a year and were closer than Paris would ever be to her family.

"What about Shelley and John? They love having you work with them."

"I can't work for the church forever. This is my chance to make a difference."

Paris knew how Andrea felt. Opportunities like this didn't come along every day, especially in a town as small as Sapphire Bay. "I admire what you want to do. The boys will be proud."

"I hope so. This is the most settled we've felt in years. I just hope I won't make their lives worse by taking on more debt."

Paris found the safety register and added their names. "The bank will only lend you money if they think the café will be a success."

Andrea sighed. "That's true. Have you heard from your mom since you opened The Flower Cottage?"

"No, thank goodness. As far as I know, she's still in Las Vegas."

"Do you think she'll come to see you?"

"Apart from her vacation, she's been busy at work. Jerry constantly flies to different cities for poker competitions, so the chance of them taking time off work to see me is remote."

"From what you've said, that's a good thing."

"It is. I'd like to have a mom who's excited for me, but it will never happen."

Andrea hugged her. "There are plenty of people in Sapphire Bay who are excited for you. Don't worry about your mom."

That was easier said than done. Especially when she'd always wanted her mother's approval—even if she was an alcoholic.

RICHARD TOOK another box into his new home. Jack was spending the morning at Shelley and John's house, getting Louie acquainted with Toto.

"Where do you want this bed, boss?"

"That's mine. Leave it in the first bedroom at the top of the stairs." Tommy and the other members of Richard's construction crew had offered to help move the heavier pieces of furniture. After the beds and a couple of dressers were removed from their tiny home, there weren't a lot of things left.

Ethan carried a box toward the kitchen. "Mabel dropped off a set of saucepans and some other kitchen things."

"She didn't have to do that."

"Believe me. There's no stopping her when she thinks she can help. Don't be surprised if she comes back with more things. She told me about a floor rug that will look perfect in your living room."

Richard pulled out his phone. "I'll call her."

"Good luck."

He didn't have to wait long for Mabel to answer her phone. After explaining how much he appreciated her help, but that he had everything he needed, she reluctantly agreed not to bring anything more to the house.

Ethan joined him on the veranda. "Do you want me to bring the last couple of boxes from your tiny home?"

Richard shook his head. "Thanks, but I'm heading to the village now. I'll put them in the truck before I clean the house."

"Sounds good. I heard you've adopted a dog from the animal shelter."

Richard opened the front gate. Small-town life had struck again. "His name's Louie. He's staying with Jack at Shelley and John's house while we move everything."

"It's just as well Diana's busy at the inn and not visiting Shelley. She keeps telling me Charlie needs another doggie friend."

"There are plenty of dogs at the animal shelter needing forever homes."

Ethan grinned. "Don't tell Diana. Good luck with the rest of the move."

"Thanks for your help."

"You're welcome. I'll see you at next week's poker game."

Tommy came out of the house with three other apprentices. "Is there anything else you want from your old house before we finish for the day?"

"No, thanks. You've done a great job."

"Having pizza for lunch was all the incentive we needed. See you next week."

Richard took another box out of his truck. After living in a tiny house for so long, he was worried he'd feel lost in his new home. But with the extra furniture Mabel and the rest of the community had dropped off, there was no chance of that.

Owning his own home was a big step toward finding his new kind of normal. As long as he took one day at a time, he knew everything would be okay.

RICHARD HAD ONLY BEEN BACK at the tiny home village for a few minutes when someone knocked on the front door. He smiled when he saw Paris standing on the veranda. Today, she wore a bright pink T-shirt with a matching scarf tied around her hair.

"I thought you'd still be at work."

"I'm closing The Flower Cottage a little earlier at the moment. Once the other businesses on Anchor Lane open, I'll stay open for longer." She looked around the tiny home. "It looks so different without your furniture."

"I was just thinking the same thing. When we arrived, I was worried the house would be too small. Today, I'm worried our new house is too big."

"You sound like Goldilocks. Once you get settled, your new house will feel just right. Are Jack and Louie still at Shelley's house?"

"They are. I'm heading there in a few minutes."

Paris took a gift-wrapped box out of her bag. "Before you leave, I wanted to give you this. I thought it might come in handy when you say goodbye to your house."

Richard frowned. "I've never said goodbye to a house before."

"Neither had I until a few years ago. I used to move around a lot. Each time I left an apartment, I felt strange. It was almost as if I was leaving before I'd finished what I was meant to do. A friend told me what she does when she moves, and it helped."

He opened the box and took out a vanilla-scented candle in a glass candleholder.

Paris handed him a box of matches. "Once everyone's gone, I light a candle and sit quietly in one of the rooms. I think about all the good memories I have of the house and the people who have been there. Before I blow out the candle, I thank the house for giving me shelter and keeping me safe." She smiled at his surprised face. "I know it sounds a little odd, but it works for me. Try it. You might be surprised by how calming it is."

"I'll give it a go. Do you want to have dinner with Jack and me tonight?"

"I'd love to, but I can't. I have an appointment with a potential client. I could stop by on my way home to see how everything has gone?"

"That sounds great. Don't worry about what time you arrive. I'll be awake."

Paris hugged him. "Enjoy the rest of the afternoon." Before she left, she smiled at a photo of Jack that was sitting on top of a box. "He looks so young."

"I took it the week after we arrived in Sapphire Bay. A lot has happened since then."

"It's amazing how doing one thing can change your entire life. I'm glad you moved to Sapphire Bay."

"So am I." Richard's heart pounded. He wanted to tell her how he felt about her, but he didn't know where to begin. "I really like you, Paris. I haven't had a girlfriend since I met Jack's mom. I have no idea if I'm doing this the right way or making a complete idiot of myself, but would you like to go out with me? On a date." His heart sank when he saw the uncertainty in her eyes.

"I really like you, too, but I'm not great at relationships. I push people away. Even though I try hard to make it work, it doesn't."

"Maybe you haven't spent time with the right person."

Paris sighed. "I like you more than I've ever liked anyone else, but I'm worried about Jack. If we start dating, he might think it will last forever. What if it doesn't?"

"He thinks you're special. Whether we're dating or not, that won't change."

Paris bit her bottom lip, then looked up at him. "Okay."

"You want to start dating?"

"I do. But if you suddenly realize something isn't right, you have to tell me."

"As long as you do the same for me, we'll be okay."

Paris grinned. "We'll either be incredibly happy or drive each other insane within a week."

He placed the candle on the windowsill and wrapped his arms around her. "I vote for the happy scenario."

"Me, too."

And with a kiss that made his toes curl, Paris showed him just how perfect they could be.

CHAPTER 17

*P*aris parked her truck outside Richard and Jack's new house. She was later than she thought she'd be, but she didn't want to rush her first meeting with a new client.

Marianne had liked the ideas Paris had shown her for her wedding. They'd even found a clever way of incorporating her fiancé's Scottish ancestry into the floral arrangements. If Marianne still liked the ideas tomorrow, she'd call The Flower Cottage and book Paris to provide the decorations for her wedding.

The lights were still on in Richard's living room, so she picked up the box beside her and walked toward the front door. He was so lucky to have found this house. It needed a little work, but it had a fantastic layout and gorgeous pieces of original architecture.

The front door opened before she'd set foot on the verandah. "I thought I heard a vehicle."

She smiled at Richard. "Sorry, I'm so late. I thought I'd be here an hour ago."

"It doesn't matter. How was your meeting?"

"The bride-to-be liked the ideas I shared with her. I'll know in the next few days if she wants me to make the bouquets and floral arrangements for her wedding. Is Jack still awake?"

Richard held open the door for her. "He went to bed half an hour ago. Would you like a hot drink or something cold?"

"Water will be fine." She looked around the living room. Large, comfy sofas sat on either side of the room with a gorgeous gray rug and coffee table between them. "This looks great. I didn't realize you had so much furniture."

"Most of it was given to us. John was replacing two sofas in The Welcome Center, so he gave us the old ones. Mabel found the rug somewhere, and Wyatt gave us two of his prints for the walls."

"Did you make the coffee table?"

"I made it with Jack. It wouldn't fit into our tiny home, so I left it at the old steamboat museum."

Paris studied the beautiful piece of furniture. "It's such a lovely honey-gold color."

"Jack oiled the wood to bring out its natural color. It was the first project we worked on together." Richard walked into the kitchen and filled two glasses with water. "I was worried about how today would go. Moving here was a big deal for Jack. He doesn't like change, but Louie made it much easier."

"He's a wonderful dog. How was Jack when you moved to Sapphire Bay?"

"The first week or two was difficult. After he'd met some new friends and discovered John's cat at The Welcome Center, he was a lot happier."

"Mr. Snuggles strikes again."

"Something like that."

Paris bent down as Louie hopped toward her. "Hello, handsome. How are you?" He leaned against her legs, enjoying every minute of their late-night cuddle. "Someone's happy to see me."

"He isn't the only one."

Richard's soft words made her smile. "For someone who's a little rusty on the dating front, you're doing a great job."

"Talking about being rusty, where would you like to go on our first official date?"

"I don't mind." Paris looked through the French doors. "We could have another picnic beside the lake?"

"What about something more adventurous?"

She didn't like the gleam in Richard's eyes. "I'm not much of a daredevil."

"Is there anything that's off limits?"

"Rock climbing and hand gliding. Other than that, I'm open to any suggestions."

"Leave it with me. Shelley said she can look after Jack tomorrow afternoon. Does that suit you?"

"That's perfect. Did you tell Shelley we're going on a date?"

Richard nodded. "Is that a problem?"

"She would see it as an opportunity." Paris smiled at Richard's confused frown. "Shelley and Andrea keep telling me how perfect you are."

"And you haven't listened to them?"

Paris wrapped her arms around his shoulders and smiled. "I am now."

Louie whimpered from beside them.

"It looks as though someone else is happy you listened." Richard rested his forehead against hers. "I don't know what the future holds, but I'd like to share it with you."

Paris closed her eyes and sighed. "I'd like that, too."

❄

RICHARD STOPPED IN FRONT OF PARIS' garage. He'd wanted their first official date to be special but, after discarding at least a dozen ideas, he still hadn't known what they could do.

That changed when he saw his friend, Levi. As well as being a genius with anything mechanical, he owned a top-of-the-line Ultra Limited Harley Davidson. With its sleek lines, custom paint, and passenger seat, it was perfect for what he had in mind. He just hoped Paris liked riding motorcycles.

Her front door opened before he could take off his helmet. With her eyes wide open, she walked toward him. "A motorcycle?"

He didn't know whether her surprise was a good sign. "You don't like them?"

"I love Harley's, but I've never seen you drive one."

He held onto Levi's helmet. "I used to own a motorcycle before I went to Afghanistan. When I returned, I sold it to pay for some medical bills."

"Was it like this one?"

Richard laughed. "Not even close. This model would have cost me more than a year's wages. It belongs to Levi Montgomery."

"Brooke's husband?"

He nodded as Paris walked around the motorcycle. "Levi hasn't taken it far, but he's planning a road trip at the end of summer."

"It's twice the size of anything I've seen."

"It's a touring bike, so it needs to be bigger than something you'd ride around town. The passenger seat has a backrest, so it's more comfortable than most." He opened one of the saddlebags and handed her a helmet. "This is Brooke's. It should fit."

When her eyes lifted to his, Richard's heart pounded. It was frightening how attracted he was to her.

"Where are we going?"

"There's a jazz festival in Bigfork. It doesn't finish until eight o'clock tonight. I thought we could drive there, enjoy some music and food, then come home before it gets too late."

"That sounds like a perfect first date. I'll get my jacket, and we can go." With an excited smile, she handed him the helmet, then hurried inside.

While he waited, he double-checked the reservation he'd made at a restaurant and called Shelley to make sure Jack and Louie were okay.

"I'm ready."

His eyebrows rose when he saw the leather jacket Paris was wearing.

She laughed and kissed his cheek. "You aren't the only person who likes motorcycles. Before I moved to Sapphire Bay, I spent a month touring around California with some friends. Our bikes weren't as amazing as this one, but it was fun."

"If you tell me you like shooting ranges, hiking, and basketball, I'll marry you next week."

"Yes, to the hiking and basketball, but I don't like guns."

He sent her a teasing smile. "I guess we're back to dating."

"For now." And with a flick of her wrist, Paris lowered the visor and waited for him to mount the bike.

The next few months would be interesting.

RICHARD REACHED for the cup of hot chocolate Paris had given him. Their date in Bigfork had gone too quickly. Over tacos and enchiladas, they'd talked about their lives, their businesses, and what was important to them.

The jazz festival was every bit as good as the advertising had promised. With three venues and non-stop entertainment, it was the perfect way to spend a Sunday afternoon. Before either of them was ready to come home, they'd joined the line of vehicles heading south and made their way back to Paris' house.

Even though he'd enjoyed her company, one thing was worrying him. And, beyond everything else, it was the most difficult to talk about.

Paris sat on the sofa beside him. "I can see why Levi and Brooke are planning a summer vacation on their motorcycle. Riding on the back of the Harley was a thousand times better than the motorcycle I drove in California."

"I'm glad you liked it. There's something I need to talk about, but I don't know where to begin."

"It sounds serious."

"It is." He tried to put his thoughts into a logical order, but it wasn't working. A part of him wished Jack was here to interrupt them, but he was still at Shelley and John's house. Taking a deep breath, he started at the beginning and hoped for the best. "My life changed after I lost my leg. The prosthetic I use makes my disability less recognizable, but it will always be there."

"You walk a lot better with your new leg."

"It's the best artificial limb on the market. Would you like to see what it looks like?"

Paris studied his face. "Are you worried about me seeing it?"

He wasn't worried. He was terrified. "Apart from Jack, my parents, and the medical staff who have been working with me, no one else has seen my stump."

"I guess it's not something you'd share with everyone." She left her cup of hot chocolate beside her and nodded. "I'd like to see it."

Sweat broke out on his brow. "There's a lot of scarring that wouldn't be there if I'd lost my leg another way. The explosion sent shrapnel everywhere and caused a lot of damage. The surgeons worked hard to keep my knee joint but, at the time, I couldn't see what difference it would make." He wiped his hands on his jeans. "Tell me if you don't like what you see."

Paris sat perfectly still. "Why do you think that could happen?"

"When I got home from Afghanistan, I felt like a failure, as if the landmine destroyed every dream I'd ever had. It took me a long time to get used to seeing my body the way it is."

"Show me your leg, Richard."

With a pounding heart, he reached for the zipper on the leg of his jeans. "Mom found a company that makes jeans and other clothing for amputees. The zipper makes it easier for me to attach my artificial limb."

Paris's hand reached out to his. "It's okay. You're an amazing man. Having a prosthetic limb doesn't change that."

"You say that now, but you haven't seen my leg or the scars on the rest of my body."

"You don't have to be perfect for me to think you're wonderful."

With trembling hands, he unzipped the lower half of his jeans and showed her the prosthetic limb.

Paris' eyes widened. "It looks like a real leg."

"BioTech Industries spends a lot of money making their prosthetics look as real as possible. The band that connects the top of the limb to my leg can be any color or material I want. It's what's underneath that's the miracle."

"Can I touch it?"

Richard moved his leg closer to Paris. He didn't have to feel the gentle caress of her fingertips to know she was impressed by what she saw. Whether she liked the rest of his leg was another story.

"It feels like normal skin. How does it work?"

"Two transmitters were implanted into my brain. One is in the frontal lobe and the other is in the cerebellum. When I move, a signal travels from the transmitters to the neural gel inside the prosthetic. The gel activates another layer of technology that replicates muscle, bone, and tendon movement. The entire process is so fast that it's almost the same as how a normal limb would react."

"That sounds complicated."

"It is. Most prosthetics are created for one type of movement. If you want to run and then walk, you have to change the prosthetic. With this technology, it doesn't matter what I want to do. The transmitter and neural gel work together to make my leg work as well as my other one."

"Do you take the prosthetic off or leave it on all day?"

"I take it off at night and use my crutches to get around." This was the part he'd been dreading. The part that made the reason for the prosthetic as tragic as the body it was attached to. "I'll show you how it attaches to my stump."

He rolled the wide band down his leg, then pushed a button on either side of the limb. "This disengages the lock inside the leg." Before he pulled the prosthetic off, he glanced at Paris. "When my first prosthetic was attached to my leg, I felt like Frankenstein."

"Did you tell your medical team how you were feeling?"

"No. They were trying to help me, but I was still coming to terms with what had happened."

"How do you feel now?"

"Usually, a lot better, but today's different. I don't want to scare you."

"You won't scare me."

Richard looked at his leg. "With the lock disengaged, all I have to do is twist the prosthetic to the right, and it comes off. Like this." He didn't dare look at Paris. "There's another gel sock over my stump. That's there for comfort and not movement."

"The bottom of your stump has to support a lot of weight."

"And sudden changes in direction and movement." He placed his hands on either side of the sock. "There are lots of deep scars on my leg and up this side of my body."

"You don't have to show me if you don't want to."

"I need you to see the real me, not the technologically enhanced version."

Paris frowned. "Do any of these technological enhancements make it easier for you to skip stones?"

His eyebrows rose. "You won the last competition. You don't need any advantage."

"That's what you say now. But what if your bionic leg gives you superpowers?"

"Like what?"

"You could be faster than a speeding bullet, more powerful than a locomotive, and able to leap tall buildings in a single bound."

Richard smiled. "That's Superman, not me."

"Have you looked in the mirror lately? You're ten times cuter than he is and much nicer."

His shoulders relaxed. "You're not worried about seeing my leg?"

"We all have things we don't want other people to know about. Your leg is important, but it's not the most important part of who you are." She placed her hand above his heart. "This is. And even if there are a few advantages to having a bionic leg, I'll love you anyway."

"You'll love me?"

Paris grinned. "That's what you get for being adorable. Now, show me your leg. Jack will be wondering where you are."

Before he thought too hard about what he was doing, Richard peeled back the sock. "What do you think?" He watched Paris' face, looking for any sign that she was disgusted by what she saw.

"It's amazing."

His eyes widened. That was the last thing he'd expected her to say. "You don't think I look like Frankenstein?"

"You're nothing like him. You've been cared for by doctors who are incredibly skilled." Her fingertips touched the jagged scars crisscrossing his leg. "Every stitch they made saved your life. *And* you've got a bionic leg. Not many people can say that."

Reaching out, he traced the shape of her jaw, the lips that were almost always smiling. "Why didn't we spend more time together when we first met?"

"We had a habit of bringing out the worst in each other. But, maybe, on some deep and meaningful level, we weren't ready for what would happen next."

"Are you ready now?"

Paris' eyes filled with tears. "I am."

Slowly, as if the world would shatter if he moved too fast, he kissed her. "So am I."

CHAPTER 18

*P*aris added another flower to the arrangement she was making for the Christmas tree farm. Although the festive season was still months away, Ben and Kylie's Christmas shop was always busy.

As soon as you walked through the big, red doors, it was easy to see why everyone loved going there. Christmas ornaments, festive decorations, and local arts and crafts filled the shelves. Paris was happy she was still making the decorations for the Christmas shop. Between the events she was decorating, and the special one-off commissions, it gave her more income.

She'd looked up when the front doorbell jingled. Her heart plummeted when she saw the beautifully dressed woman who'd walked into The Flower Cottage.

"Mom? What are you doing here?"

Donna Haynes walked across the store in high heels made for a fashion runway, not a flower shop in rural Montana. "Don't be annoyed, darling. I had to come and see your little store for myself."

"I thought you had to go back to work after your vacation in Las Vegas?"

The dismissive sound coming from her mother's mouth didn't bode well for her job. "I can't work for a company who don't appreciate the skills I bring to my job."

Paris sighed. "They fired you, didn't they?"

"I chose to leave. They had no respect for their employees."

Which meant she'd been fired.

"Aren't you going to give me a hug?" Donna opened her arms wide. "I've come a long way to see my little girl."

Reluctantly, Paris walked toward her. "It's good to see you."

Donna's arms gripped her like a vice. "I knew you would appreciate a visit. The last few days have been so hard. Jerry doesn't understand why I left my job. He has no appreciation for the little things that make a career so much more enjoyable."

Paris wiggled free of her mom's arms. "What little things?"

"Oh, you know. It's nice to be welcomed into work each morning with a smile. My manager was so grumpy. All she ever did was complain about my work. Anyone would think I didn't have better options available to me."

Maybe it wasn't as bad as Paris thought. "You have another job?"

"Not yet, but I'm working on it." Donna looked around the store. "This is a lovely little cottage, but what's happening next door? The parking spaces are full of construction trucks."

"The cottages along Anchor Lane are being remodeled. In a few weeks, the construction crew will be working on the third cottage and father away from here. That should make finding a park a lot easier."

Her mom wandered into the display area and studied a gift basket Paris had made. "This is so cute. It reminds me of a basket my sister made for a baby shower we went to. You must have inherited your artistic streak from Aunt Cynthia."

If anyone had been listening to their conversation, they'd think her mom had complimented her. But Aunt Cynthia's career as an artist had earned her more disdain from her family than anything else.

Instead of letting her mom's words upset her, Paris took a box of ornaments off the workroom table and unpacked them. "How long are you staying in Sapphire Bay?"

Donna's smile sent shivers down Paris' back. "I haven't made any definite plans yet. Jerry is in Atlantic City at a poker tournament. He could be there for two or three weeks."

"You aren't staying here for that long, are you?"

"I don't have anywhere else I need to be. Don't frown. It will give you premature wrinkles."

Her mom couldn't stay in Sapphire Bay for that long. Even now, Paris didn't know whether or not her mom was drunk. All it would take was one night of binge drinking, and the entire community would know she was an alcoholic.

"Don't you have to go back to Los Angeles and look for another job?"

Donna shrugged. "It won't take me long to find something else. Besides, Jerry is doing well. With what he earns from the poker tournament, we won't have to worry about money for a while."

If Paris had put aside a dollar every time her mom said that, she'd be a millionaire. "I still think it's worthwhile looking for another job. You can't count on Jerry's income to pay your bills."

"You always were such a negative little thing. Jerry and I might have had a few rough patches, but we always have enough to live comfortably." Donna picked up a glass Christmas ornament. "These are sweet. Where did you find them?"

"A man in Great Falls makes them." Paris watched her mom move around the store. Why would she want to stay in Sapphire Bay? She'd never visited for more than a few days. "Where are you staying while you're here?"

It was Donna's turn to frown. "With you, of course. I looked online for somewhere to stay, but there's nothing available. You don't mind, do you?"

Paris sighed. "You know what happens when you stay with me. It won't work, mom."

"We haven't spent any time together for ages. I thought this would be the ideal opportunity to heal old wounds."

"Have you stopped drinking?"

Donna's face hardened. "I've told you before. I don't have a drinking problem."

"You're an alcoholic, Mom. You need professional help."

The front door opened and Andrea stepped inside. "Oops. Am I interrupting something?"

Andrea had met Paris' mom on her last disastrous visit. Donna had only stayed for two days, but it had felt like a lifetime. "It's okay. Do you remember my mom? She just flew in from Los Angeles."

"It's nice to see you again, Mrs. Haynes."

"You make me feel so old when you call me that. Please, call me Donna."

Andrea's smile didn't waver. "Isn't The Flower Cottage gorgeous? Paris has done such a great job of setting up the business."

"It's very… quaint." Donna glanced at another display. "I wouldn't have thought there was much point in opening a flower shop in the middle of nowhere."

Even Andrea's unflappable feathers bristled at Donna's

words. "We're hardly in the middle of nowhere, Mrs. Haynes. A lot of people are moving to Sapphire Bay and the number of tourists has tripled. People come here to experience the best small-town life can offer."

"I prefer a little more activity."

"You won't be staying long, then?"

Paris cleared her throat. She'd better interrupt their conversation before Andrea marched her mom out of town. "We're still discussing how long mom's staying."

The look Donna sent her was glacial. "If I can't stay with you, I won't have any choice but to leave."

"You can stay with me for a few days. I'll ask if anyone else in town has some accommodation available."

Donna stuck her nose in the air. "While you're doing that, I'll drive to your house and unpack. It's a little colder here than in California."

Andrea stepped out of Donna's way. "If you need another jacket, the general store has a few options."

She knew as well as Paris that her mom wouldn't shop anywhere that didn't sell designer labels.

"I'll keep that in mind." And with the same speed that she arrived, Donna left the store.

Andrea closed the door behind her. "I'm sorry I was rude to your mom, but she annoys me so much. How can she not see how amazing you are?"

Paris sighed. "Mom uses alcohol to cope with her life. It must be difficult to see anything amazing when your brain has been taken over by an addiction."

"You're more forgiving than I would be."

If Andrea knew how much hurt and damage her mom's alcoholism had caused, she'd realize it wasn't forgiveness that motivated her. It was guilt. For years, Paris blamed herself for not taking care of her mom. For leaving home as soon as she could to get away from her drunken rages. It wasn't until she moved to Sapphire Bay that Paris realized she shouldn't feel guilty. She'd done everything she could to help her mom.

"I can't let her sleep in her car."

"Why don't you call The Lakeside Inn? They might have a spare room your mom can use."

"That's a good idea."

Andrea hugged her. "It's a *great* idea. I know you love her, but does she realize how destructive she is?"

"Mom thinks the world is against her. It colors everything she thinks and does, and makes it hard for her to relate to anyone. With everything that's happening, the last thing I need is a visit from her."

"I don't want to suggest this, but I'm going to. Would you consider asking her to leave?"

"I can't. She's my mom."

"In that case, you'll need all the help you can get. You call The Lakeside Inn and I'll contact Jackie. Between us, we'll try and limit the amount of time your mom has with you. As long as I don't lose my temper, we'll be fine."

For Andrea to lose her temper, things had to be really bad. She was the most easy-going person Paris knew, but Donna would try the patience of a saint. "Are you sure you want to spend time with Mom? She can be overwhelming sometimes."

"Your mom is *always* overwhelming. It's just as well you don't live in the same town as her. But that's not why I came to see you. Guess what?"

"You've found the perfect baby shower gift for Kylie?"

"Not yet, but I've narrowed down a few options. I came to tell you I've submitted my loan application to the bank. In a few days, I should know whether I have enough money to open a café in the next cottage."

"That's fantastic! I'm so proud of you."

"I hope the loans officer is as positive as you are. I'm terrified I'm making the biggest mistake of my life."

Paris hugged Andrea. "I thought the same thing before I signed the lease on my cottage. Sometimes, even after you've done all your research, you have to take a leap of faith and believe it's meant to be. If you need anything, just ask."

Andrea pointed to Paris' cell phone. "I need you to call The Lakeside Inn before your mom decides to move here. I'll be in touch with a cunning plan to keep the two of you apart."

"I don't know whether to thank you or be incredibly worried."

"You might need to do both. Especially if your mom has other ideas about what she wants to do."

AFTER HE'D FINISHED WORK, Richard brought Jack to the basketball court behind The Welcome Center. It was a great evening to be in the fresh air, especially after his busy afternoon.

He bounced the basketball closer to Jack. "I'm setting myself up for a big shot."

Jack rubbed his hands down the sides of his shorts. "I'm ready."

Louie yapped happily from the sideline.

With more enthusiasm than skill, he drove the ball forward. Jack stuck to him like glue, doing a great job of making Richard's job harder.

The only way he was going to score was to go for a three-pointer. He dodged to the right, pivoted, and then threw the ball into the air.

With a heavy thud, it hit the backboard and careened

across the court. Like a streak of lightning, Jack grabbed the ball and threw it toward the hoop.

Unlike Richard's shot, it whooshed through the net.

"Yeah!" Jack yelled. "That's three points for me. Bad luck, Dad."

"How do you do that? You're half my height, but you get the ball in the hoop more than I do."

Jack grinned. "You have to practice more."

He was probably right.

"There's Paris." Jack waved and pointed across the court. Before Richard knew what he was doing, Jack sprinted toward her.

Today, Paris was wearing a bright orange dress and a black jacket. Compared to some of her other clothes, it was almost demure. By the time Richard joined them, Jack was admiring the flowers she was holding.

Paris smiled. "Hi, Richard. I only caught the last few minutes of your game, but I was impressed."

"Jack played really well. I haven't been on a basketball court in months and it shows."

"You played good, Dad." Jack looked toward the wire fence. "I'd better get Louie. I could teach him how to play basketball, just like us."

While Jack rushed across the court to rescue Louie, Richard looked at Paris' flowers. The pale purple roses weren't like anything he'd seen before. "They're an unusual color."

"A friend of Pastor John's is planning a big anniversary party for his parents. His mom carried a bouquet of purple roses when she got married. I'm hoping these roses match the ones she had." Paris looked at his legs. "You're wearing shorts."

"Someone told me I'd never be happy unless I embraced who I am. Since my accident, I've been hiding behind my

171

clothes, trying to look normal." If Paris saw the blush on his face, she didn't say anything. "It was time to change that."

Paris smiled. "I'm glad you did. Your legs look incredible."

"Thanks. No one's ever told me I have great legs."

"I guess there's a first time for everything. I'd better take the flowers inside. I'm meeting Pastor John's friend in a few minutes."

"Are you doing anything tonight?"

Her smile disappeared. "Mom arrived unexpectedly today. She's staying with me for a few days."

"When was the last time you saw her?"

"About a year ago. I feel bad that I don't make more of an effort to see her, but being around her is really hard."

Even while she was sitting up her business, he hadn't seen Paris looking so stressed. "Will you be all right?"

"I hope so. In two days, Katie has a bedroom available at The Lakeside Inn. I reserved it for Mom, but she doesn't want to stay there."

That surprised Richard. Since it had been remodeled, there had been nothing but high praise for the high-quality accommodation it offered. "Has she seen the inn?"

Paris nodded. "It's just Mom. She wants to stay with me, so nothing will change her mind."

"Why don't you bring her to my house for dinner tonight? I'll put on the barbecue and cook my world-famous marinated steak with grilled corn salad."

"I couldn't do that to you and Jack. Mom can be unpredictable."

"Because of her drinking?"

"Even when she isn't drinking, she isn't the same as most people."

He wasn't going to leave Paris with someone she didn't feel safe with. Even if it was her mother. "Have dinner with us. If your mom's around other people, it might make her react differently to what you say."

"Okay, we'll come. What time would you like us to arrive?"

"Is six-thirty okay? It won't take long to cook everything."

"That's fine. Thanks for inviting us."

"Don't worry about your mom. With Jack and Louie to keep her company, she won't have anything to complain about."

"I hope you're right. I'll see you soon." Paris waved to Jack as she hurried toward The Welcome Center.

Richard walked toward Jack and Louie. It wasn't the dinner he'd imagined when he'd bought the steak, but it would be interesting. Paris didn't talk about her mom. Tonight, he might understand why.

CHAPTER 19

"*It* was nice of your friend to invite us to dinner," Donna said from the passenger seat of Paris' truck. "You haven't mentioned his name before."

"I didn't get to know Richard until I decided to lease the cottage on Anchor Lane. He managed the construction crew that was doing the work." Paris stopped outside Richard's house. "He moved into his new home the same weekend I opened The Flower Cottage. He wants to do some remodeling, but it's early days yet."

Donna unbuckled her seatbelt. "Jerry and I have been talking about making some changes to our house but, with everything else that's happening, we haven't had a chance to talk to an interior designer."

Jerry must be earning more money than Paris realized. Interior designers in Los Angeles didn't come cheap, and her mom had expensive taste. But, even if he was making lots of money on the poker circuit, it wasn't guaranteed income. With her mom unemployed, they could get themselves into serious debt.

Paris took a box of desserts off the back seat and led her mom through the front gate. "Richard's son's name is Jack."

"Yes, yes, I know. He's nine years old and has a dog called Louie."

At least her mom remembered that. She just hoped she remembered to be on her best behavior.

The front door swung open. Jack and Louie bounded down the steps. "Hi, Paris and Paris' mom," he said with a grin. "I'm Jack."

Reaching out, Donna shook Jack's hand. "It's a pleasure to meet you and your little dog."

Paris' eyebrows rose. Louie was leaning against her mom's legs, looking blissfully up at her as if she was his best friend.

"You're a friendly little dog."

Jack patted Louie's back. "He only has three legs. There was a bad accident and the doctor had to take one of them off. Just like my dad."

Donna frowned. "Your dad was in an accident?"

"He was in the Army and a landmine went boom, and he almost died. Do you like corn? It's my favorite vegetable 'cos it's not green."

Instead of being overwhelmed by Jack's zigzagging mind, Donna simply nodded. "I'm a big fan of corn, too. My mother used to make corn fritters when I was a little girl."

"We haven't had those."

Richard walked onto the veranda and joined them. He shook Donna's hand. "I'm Richard. It's nice to meet you Mrs. Haynes."

"Please, call me Donna. Your son is charming."

Richard blinked. Paris wasn't sure what he was thinking, but it was probably what most people thought before they got to know her mom. She could be incredibly polite, funny,

175

and witty. Until something happened. And then she was someone you didn't want to be around.

"Welcome to Sapphire Bay, Donna. Come inside before you get cold."

While her mom said something about how different the temperature was in Montana, Paris patted Louie.

"We've got ice cream for dessert," Jack whispered.

Paris showed him the box. "I bought some yummy treats, too."

"It will be like a party."

She wished she shared Jack's enthusiasm. "I hope so. Let's go inside." With an impending sense of doom, she followed Richard and her mom into the house. Hopefully, Donna would be on her best behavior and everything would be fine. If not, Paris might be the one checking into The Lakeside Inn.

RICHARD WALKED into the living room with a cup of coffee for Donna. The barbecue had been a success and dessert was delicious. Apart from Paris being on edge the entire time, it could have been a normal family dinner.

Donna smiled as he placed the cup beside her. "Thank you. I enjoy a nice coffee at the end of a meal. Are you enjoying your ice cream sundae, Jack?"

"It's yummy. There's a candy store in town that sells amazing ice cream. Dad takes me there all the time."

"You're a lucky boy."

"That's what Grandma says. She's coming to visit us soon."

"That will be nice. Is she staying with you and your dad?"

Paris's hand tightened around her coffee cup.

Jack nodded. "We made a bedroom for her. It has pink

cushions and a fluffy blanket on the end of the bed. Louie likes to rub his whiskers on the blanket, but dad tells him not to."

"That's a very sensible thing to teach Louie. He's a cute dog, but your grandma won't want his hair everywhere. It's nice she has her own bedroom. It must make her feel wanted."

Paris' gaze shot to her mom.

Before Paris said something she might regret, Richard jumped into the conversation. "When mom arrives, she'll be surprised by the changes in Sapphire Bay. We have a lot of construction happening around town."

"Paris told me you're in charge of the people remodeling the cottages on Anchor Lane. That must be a rewarding job."

"It is, especially when we're employing local people. A few years ago, it was a different story. A lot of older people and families looking for an alternative lifestyle lived here. Now, young people are living and working here, and businesses are thinking of relocating to Sapphire Bay."

"We have plenty of events, too," Paris added. "There's an amazing Christmas program, farmers' markets, and fishing competitions. There's something for everyone."

Jack licked the last of his ice cream off his spoon. "My favorite things are the boat races and the strawberry festival. I like strawberries."

Donna nodded. "They're very good for you." She looked at Richard and smiled. "Would you mind if I added some cold water to my coffee? It's a little hot."

He started to rise. "I can do it for you."

"Don't be silly. You're enjoying your coffee. I know where the kitchen is."

Paris left her cup on the table. "I'll do it for you, Mom."

"I can do it myself, but thank you for the offer." Before Paris could reply, Donna left the room.

Richard frowned. "Is everything all right?"

Paris rubbed her forehead. "My head is pounding. I'll see if mom's ready to go home in a few minutes."

"I've got some Tylenol, if that would help?"

"It's okay. I've got plenty at home. I'll just go and see Mom."

Richard stopped her before she walked into the kitchen. "What's wrong?"

"Mom often adds bourbon to her coffee," she whispered. "I don't want her drinking around Jack."

"Do you want me to check on her?"

"I'll do it. Thanks for making tonight much better than it would have been." And, with a sad smile, she walked into the kitchen.

Richard hadn't had a close relationship with anyone who was an alcoholic. He couldn't begin to understand what Paris and her mom's lives must be like, but he wanted to help.

The only problem was, where did he start?

PARIS WALKED into the kitchen expecting the worst. She wasn't disappointed.

"What are you doing, Mom?"

Donna didn't even look embarrassed that she'd been caught. "I'm adding a little something to my coffee."

"I asked you before we left not to drink alcohol while we're here."

"I haven't had anything to drink all night. A sparrow couldn't get drunk on the amount of bourbon in this cup."

"That's not the point. When you drink, you get mean and nasty. I don't want Richard or Jack to see you when you're like that."

"Is that why you haven't invited me to Sapphire Bay? You're embarrassed to have me anywhere near you?"

Paris took a deep breath and counted to ten. "You keep promising you'll change. But, each time I see you, you're doing the same thing over and over again. That's why I haven't asked you to stay with me."

"I've tried to drink less, but it isn't easy."

"That's why you need professional help. But you refuse to go into an addiction program."

Donna's eyes filled with tears. "I don't need strangers telling me how to fix my life."

"You need someone to help you," Paris said firmly. She hardened her heart at the sight of her mom's tears. They were Donna's secret weapon. She'd use them mercilessly if she thought they'd give her what she wanted. "For most of my life, I've tried to make it easier for you to give up alcohol. I stayed with you when you were detoxing. I made sure there was no alcohol in the house, and I kept your drinking friends away. But nothing changed."

"You aren't my mother. I've never needed a babysitter."

"If you stopped drinking, you'd see the harm you're doing to yourself and everyone around you."

"I'm not hurting anyone. Jerry loves me. He—"

"Jerry is an enabler." Paris's voice trembled with emotion. "He uses you to support his gambling addiction. Without your regular income, he would be homeless."

Donna straightened her shoulders. "Jerry is my rock. He loves me regardless of whether or not I drink."

Paris rubbed her hand across her forehead. "I don't want to argue with you, Mom. We should go home."

Donna picked up her bag. "Now that you've upset me, you want to pretend nothing's wrong? I can't believe how hurtful you are. You haven't returned my calls or wanted to see me for the last three years. When I come to see you, you

179

can't bear to be around me. I see so little of you that I might as well not have a daughter."

Richard opened the kitchen door. He took one look at Paris' face and stood beside her. "I overheard some of what you were saying and called a friend. John has a spare bed in The Welcome Center. Do you want your mom to stay there tonight, Paris?"

She looked at her mom and felt as though her entire world had collapsed. It had been so long since she'd had to be strong around her that she'd forgotten how difficult it was. "I think that's for the best. I'm sorry, Mom, but I can't do this anymore."

"This is ridiculous. You're acting like a spoiled child."

"That's enough," Richard said in a low voice.

Donna crossed her arms in front of her chest. "If I'm not wanted, I don't have a choice, do I?"

Richard wrapped his arm around Paris' waist. "If you give me your house keys, I'll take your mom home, pick up her things, and get her settled into the center. Jack's watching TV with Louie."

"Will you be okay?"

"Oh, for goodness sakes. He's a grown man. Of course, he'll be okay." And with those parting words, Donna stormed out of the kitchen.

Richard hugged her. "I won't be too long. Give me a call if you need me."

Paris nodded. "Thank you."

"You're welcome. Lock the door behind me."

After Richard and her mom left, Paris returned to the kitchen. Picking up her mom's coffee, she tipped it down the sink. She wished her mother was different and, that one day, she'd have the courage to stop drinking. But until that day came, Paris couldn't give her what she wanted.

"Has your mom gone home?" Jack asked from the kitchen doorway.

Paris nodded. "Your dad's dropping her off and coming straight back. Are you enjoying the movie?"

"It's awesome. Do you want to watch it with me?

She wrapped her arm around Jack's shoulders, taking strength from his happiness. "I'd love to. Where's Louie?"

"He fell asleep on the sofa. He snores, just like dad."

For the first time that night, Paris smiled. "I didn't know your dad snores."

"He sounds like a freight train." They walked into the living room and Jack flopped onto the sofa. "I'm watching *Shrek*. Have you seen it?"

"I watched it a long time ago. I like it, too." With her legs curled under her, Paris tried to relax. But, all she could hear was her mother's voice, telling her she might as well not have a daughter.

CHAPTER 20

*R*ichard was glad to finally be home. He walked into the living room and smiled. Jack was watching the end of *Shrek*, and Paris was sound asleep on the sofa. With her long lashes shadowing her cheeks, and jet-black hair hanging loose around her shoulders, she could have been Snow White waiting for her Prince Charming.

Except he was no prince, and rescuing anyone from their wicked mother wasn't something he wanted to repeat. Especially after what had happened tonight.

He'd felt sick when he heard what Donna was telling Paris in the kitchen. Throughout their meal, he'd ignored Donna's backhanded compliments, the comments that must have twisted like a knife inside her daughter's heart. He'd moved the conversation onto safer topics and hoped Paris knew how much he wanted to protect her.

By the end of the night, the only thing he could do was make sure Donna had somewhere else to stay.

Silently, he moved across the room. Louie lifted his head from Jack's lap and gave a deep doggy sigh. When Jack saw him, Richard held a finger to his lips and pointed at Paris.

Jack nodded and wiggled off the sofa. "She missed the best part," he whispered.

"Paris can watch the rest of the movie another day. How about I put you to bed?"

"Okay." Jack and Louie followed him upstairs. "Can we see Paris' mom tomorrow?"

"I don't know if she'll still be here, but she enjoyed having dinner with us. How was Paris after we left?"

"She enjoyed the movie. She likes spending time with us."

"How do you feel about her?"

Jack walked into the bathroom and took his toothbrush out of a cup. "She's nice. Paris is always happy, except tonight. She looked sad when her mom left."

"Sometimes it isn't easy loving someone."

"Like Shrek. He was big and green, and pretended to be mean. But he was only angry because he thought no one liked him. Fiona showed him he was perfect, just the way he was."

Richard handed Jack a towel. Paris had done the same thing. Her quirky sense of humor, her kindness, and her patience had touched something deep inside him. He wasn't big and green, but he had given up on finding someone who would love him for who he had become.

After he finished in the bathroom, Jack climbed into bed and Louie settled beside him.

Richard kissed his son's forehead. "I love you, buddy."

"Love you, too. Can you turn on my night-light?"

"No problem. I'll see you in the morning."

"Okay. Dad?"

"Yes?"

"Tell Paris to remember Fiona."

"Fiona?"

"From *Shrek*. She thought she had to hide who she was for people to like her. But Shrek loved her best when she was herself. It didn't matter if she was a normal girl or green like him."

Richard took a moment for his son's words to sink in. "I'll tell her. Have wonderful dreams."

"I will."

Before he went downstairs, he took a blanket out of the linen closet. Listening to Paris' mom talk about her relationship with her daughter made him realize how lucky he was. Through their own challenges, his parents had loved and supported him. Although his dad wasn't here anymore, they'd shared a special bond that Richard would always treasure.

How Paris had survived her childhood with an alcoholic mother was beyond him. But, she'd not only survived, she'd created a completely different life from her mom's.

When he walked into the living room, Paris was still asleep. As he draped the blanket over her, she opened her eyes.

"Hi," she said sleepily. "Is Mom okay?"

"She's fine. It took a few minutes to get her settled into The Welcome Center, but she seemed happy with the room."

"That's good." Slowly, Paris sat upright. "Where's Jack?"

"He's in bed. He asked me to remind you about Fiona."

She frowned and then smiled. "My favorite part of *Shrek* is when Fiona turns into her true self, knowing Shrek will love her whatever decision she makes. Do you think Jack's trying to tell me something?"

"Knowing my son, anything's possible."

She rubbed her eyes and yawned. "Thank you for looking after mom. I feel really bad for not taking her home, but she would have kept drinking…" Her eyes widened. "I forgot about the bourbon. I should call Pastor John and warn him—"

"It's okay. Donna gave me the flask and a bottle of

bourbon before we left your house. They're sitting on your kitchen counter."

Paris sighed. "I'm sorry about tonight. You must think I'm heartless to want mom to stay somewhere else."

Richard sat beside her. "I don't think you're heartless. You've spent most of your life living with an alcoholic. At some point, you had to set boundaries. Otherwise, you could have ended up like her. What did you do when you were younger?"

"Grandma looked after me. Whenever I walked to her house, she always made me a meal and let me stay with her. If Mom realized I wasn't at home, she'd pick me up. If she'd been drinking, Grandma would tell her to come back when she was sober and could look after me."

"When did you realize your mom was an alcoholic?"

"I think I was about eight years old. None of the other children in my class had mothers who drank until they couldn't walk straight. When mom forgot to buy groceries or fill out the forms for school, I made excuses for her. Later on, I felt like I was the adult in our relationship and mom was the child."

"What about your dad?"

"Grandma said he left because of mom's drinking. I was really young when he left, so I don't remember anything about him." Paris' blue eyes were clouded with worry. "Welcome to my dysfunctional family."

"It could be worse."

"How?"

"If your life was different, you might never have come to Sapphire Bay, and we wouldn't have met."

Tears filled her eyes. "You found the silver lining."

"I learned from the best." Richard wrapped her in a hug. "Whatever happens, you'll always have Jack and me to look after you."

"What if mom doesn't stop drinking?"

"That's her decision. She knows there are consequences to what she's doing."

"I'm not sure she does." Paris rested her head against his chest. "What would I do without you?"

Richard kissed the top of her head. "You don't have to worry about that. I'm not going anywhere."

THE NEXT MORNING, Paris walked into The Welcome Center, nervous about what could happen. She'd hardly slept last night and, when she had, her dreams were full of the times her mom was drunk.

She didn't want to live without her, but they couldn't carry on like this.

Pastor John walked into the reception area. "Hi, Paris. You're here early."

"I wanted to see Mom before I open The Flower Cottage. Thank you for finding a room for her."

"It was no problem. We keep a room for emergency accommodation, and no one needed it. If you want to talk about what happened, I'm here for you."

Despite giving herself a stern talk about staying strong and not letting her emotions override what she wanted to say, Paris' eyes filled with tears. "Thank you."

John wrapped his arm around her shoulders and led her into his office. "Sit here for a minute. I'll get you a glass of water."

By the time he returned, she'd wiped her face and steadied her racing heart.

"Feeling better?"

"I am. I was awake for most of the night. If I don't get enough sleep, I get emotional."

"Why didn't you sleep?"

"Did Richard tell you why my mom's here?"

"He said she'd arrived unexpectedly and needed some-where to stay. Before Donna was given a room, we asked her the same questions we ask everyone who stays here. That's when she told us she has a drinking problem. Is that part of the reason you're upset?"

Paris nodded. "I've spent most of my life looking after her, but I'm tired of worrying about whether she'll be all right. I've tried getting her help. I've ignored the lies she tells to cover up her drinking. I've given her money to get her life back on track, but nothing helps. It never will until she stops drinking. I came here to tell her I can't see her until she's sober."

"How do you think she'll react?"

"She won't like it." Paris blew her nose. "I used to worry I'd end up like her. I'd joke that my superpower was pushing people away. Every relationship I had was based on how fast I thought I could leave. Until now, the only person I never gave up on was Mom."

"That's because you love her. Donna said she lives in Santa Fe. I'll ask her if she wants me to suggest a counsellor she could see."

"Thank you. I'd better let you get back to work."

"Do you want me to come with you?"

"No. It's better if I see her on my own. I appreciate you talking to me."

"I'm glad I was here. Remember you aren't alone, Paris. More people than you realize are dealing with addictions."

She took a deep breath and picked up her bag. "I'll remember."

Now all she had to do was say goodbye to her mom.

❅

WITH A POUNDING HEART, Paris stood outside her mom's room. She didn't know how she'd tell her she couldn't see her anymore but, for her own sanity, she had to do it.

"Paris?"

She turned and looked at her mom. "I just knocked on your door."

"I've been in the dining room having breakfast. I met some nice people who have moved here from Oregon."

As usual, her mom looked impeccable. The jeans and shirt she was wearing wouldn't have been out of place on Sunset Boulevard. "You look nice."

"I try my best. Your dress is pretty."

"You sent it to me last year." The cherry red rockabilly dress was one of her favorites, mostly because her mom had taken the time to buy it for her.

"I thought it looked familiar." Donna smiled, but Paris could see the strain it was taking to appear normal. Her mom must have been dreading this conversation as much as she was. "I spoke to Jerry last night. He wants me to come to Atlantic City."

If she did that, it would be the end of any counseling her mom might have considered. "Are you going?"

"I don't know. I'm still thinking about it."

"That's good." Paris looked down the corridor. "There is a small seating area at the end of the hallway. Do you want to sit there for a few minutes?"

Donna shook her head. "I'd prefer to speak here. I'm sorry about last night. I didn't mean to upset you."

"I've been thinking about what happened, too. I overreacted when I saw you adding bourbon to your coffee. It's just—"

"You don't have to say it. I know how hard it's been for you. How hard I've made your life. When I walked past Jack on my way out of Richard's home, I realized I was repeating what I'd done when you were his age."

Paris didn't know what to say, so she remained silent.

"Jack's an intelligent little boy with so much enthusiasm for everything he does. I can't remember what you were like. I don't know what you enjoyed eating or what your favorite stories were. I have no idea who your friends were or whether you liked school. Last night, I learned more about Jack than I remember about you."

Paris looked over her shoulder, hoping no one overheard them. "It doesn't matter."

"It does. If it weren't for your grandma, I don't know what would have happened to you. At the time, I was so caught up in my own life that I didn't care about anything except my next drink. You shouldn't have had to live through that."

"I turned out okay."

"You turned out more than okay," her mom said softly. "I'm very proud of you, even if I've never told you."

Paris clenched her fists, trying to focus on anything other than the tears building behind her eyes. "I wanted to be a florist because of you. Do you remember the rose we used to take to each of our apartments?"

Donna looked as though she was trying hard to remember. "What was it like?"

"It was a miniature red rose. Each time we moved, you'd carefully pack it in the car, making sure it didn't tip over. You said Dad gave it to you on the day I was born and that we should cherish it. We didn't have a lot of things, but we always had the rose."

"What happened to it?"

"When I came home from one of my visits to Grandma's, I thought it had died. You'd forgotten to water it. I asked

189

Grandma how I could save it and she bought some potting mix and fertilizer. We looked after it at her house. By some miracle, it survived. I planted it in my garden when I moved here."

"It's still alive?"

Paris nodded. "It's the only link I have to my father. I thought if he'd bought you the rose, it must mean he loved us. Loved me." She took a deep breath and let it out slowly. "It wasn't until I started working at Blooming Lovely that I realized how important flowers are in people's lives. They make people happy. I wanted desperately to be happy, but something inside me was broken. It wasn't until I met my friends in Sapphire Bay, and talked to the customers who came into Kylie's flower shop, that I started changing. For the first time in years, I was happy. And it terrified me."

"Oh, baby. I'm so sorry."

"I can't go back to how things used to be. I can't keep worrying about whether you'll kill yourself in a car accident or hurt someone else. I don't want to think about whether you're spending your money on alcohol or paying your bills, or if you're lying in a gutter somewhere, sleeping off a hangover. I can't do any of it. If I do, I'll go back to how I used to be."

Tears fell from her mom's eyes. "I want you to be happy, too. Which is why I've made some decisions." She wiped her face and lifted her chin. "I can't see you for a while. I need to decide how I want to live, and who I want to be. I can't do that when I rely on you to rescue me. I don't know where I'll go, but I won't be staying in Sapphire Bay. I'm sorry if you're upset, but it's the only way I'll know if I can make it on my own."

Hot tears clouded Paris' vision. Even though her mom had come to the same conclusion, it was difficult to hear.

For the first time in years, she hugged her mom. "I love you. I hope everything works out for you."

"I love you, too, baby. Keep watering the rose. One day, I'll come back and see it." With a deep, shuddering breath, Donna stepped away from Paris. "Now leave before my ugly tears arrive. You have a business to open, and I need to pack my bags."

She gave her mom another quick hug, and then hurried out of The Welcome Center. By the time she reached her truck, Paris was sobbing so hard she didn't know if she would ever stop.

CHAPTER 21

*R*ichard held Paris' hand as they walked around Flathead Lake. Jack was in front of them, playing fetch with Louie.

The last week had been hard for Paris. Between her mom leaving, and finding new clients for her business, she'd been through a roller coaster of emotions.

He stopped to pick up a flat pebble that would make a perfect skipping stone. "I spoke to Mom the other day. She's coming to stay with Jack and me in two weeks. Would you like to meet her?"

Paris' eyes sparkled as brightly as the sun's reflection off the lake. "I'd love to. Especially if she likes telling people stories about your childhood."

"You can't discover my secrets that way."

"Don't be too sure. Grandma used to say, 'Show me a child at seven, and I'll show you the man.' I wonder if that's as true for you as it was for me?"

"I don't know, but Jack hasn't changed much over the last couple of years. He's still as curious about the world as ever."

"Dad! Look at this." Jack rushed toward them with Louie yapping at his heels. "They're gemstones."

Richard looked at the small, blue rocks. "They're unusual, that's for sure." He showed them to Paris. "What do you think they are, Jack?"

"My teacher showed us some pictures of gemstones people have found in Montana. They look like one of the stones, but I don't remember what they're called."

"I'll have a look on the Internet." Paris took out her phone and started her search.

Jack handed Richard another blue stone. "Did you know Montana is called the treasure state? That's because people have found gold, silver, and even diamonds, all over the place."

"I didn't know that. Where did you find the stones?"

"Over here." Jack ran back to the edge of the water. "They were around here somewhere."

"I've found something on the Internet." Paris ran to catch up with them. "Jack's right. The stones look remarkably like sapphires. Apparently, they were first discovered in Montana in the 1860s. In the 1990s, commercial mining operations found several million carats of sapphires, mostly in south-eastern Montana." She showed Jack and Richard the pictures on the website. "They come in all sorts of colors, but the blue ones are the most valuable."

Jack's eyes widened. "I've found real treasure. Just like a pirate."

Paris nodded. "It looks like it."

"We have to search for more." Jack spun back to where he thought he'd found the stones.

Richard looked at Paris. "Do you want to do a little treasure hunting before dinner?"

"Why not? You never know—Jack might have found enough stones to buy a space rocket and fly to the moon."

"Just like in my books," he said excitedly. "But if I can't buy a rocket, a new Legos set will be okay."

Richard knew which set he wanted, too. "While we're looking for more sapphires, I have a question for everyone."

Jack's hand was in the water, picking any small stones out of the lake. "What is it?"

"I spoke to Mr. Bennett, the Chief Executive of BioTech Industries. His company has started designing prosthetic limbs for dogs. It could be a long time before they're available, but Louie would be able to join their trial team if we want him to."

Jack frowned. "Does that mean he'd have a leg like yours?"

"Sort of like mine, but designed for him."

Paris frowned. "Are you joking?"

"It's true. At the moment, they're running design simulations to work out how the prosthetic could be fitted onto a dog's limb."

"Why do you want Louie to have a prosthetic leg?" Paris asked.

Richard would have thought the answer was obvious. "It will stop his other joints from being damaged from the extra impact they have to handle. Walking and running will be a lot easier, and people won't stare at him when we're away from home."

"Did people stare at you when you came home from Afghanistan?"

Paris' question surprised him. "They did, but they tried to hide it. I was treated differently, even when I was wearing jeans and using crutches."

"We used to go to the front of the line when Dad was in his wheelchair." Jack handed him another small stone. "This one isn't blue, but it looks pretty."

"You remember what happened?"

"It was cool. Now we have to wait like everyone else." Jack sounded disappointed.

Richard held onto the stone while Paris joined Jack in the search for more treasure. "So, what does everyone think about a new leg for Louie?"

Jack patted Louie's back when he joined them in the water. "What do you think, boy? Do you want a new leg?"

Louie's happy yap made Jack smile. "He said, yes."

Paris didn't look quite so certain. "Are there any issues with implanting a processor into an animal?"

"It only works in conjunction with the gel in the prosthetic. The worst that can happen is that it has to be removed."

"Will it hurt Louie?" Jack asked.

Richard shook his head. "He won't feel the processor. The prosthetic leg will feel different until he gets used to wearing it, but it won't hurt."

"I vote yes, too," Jack said enthusiastically. "Then he'll be Louie, the wonder dog!"

Paris added another stone to the ones in Richard's hand. "If everyone else is happy, I'll vote for the new leg for Louie, too. But, either way, he's still a wonder dog."

And that, Richard decided, was why he loved her so much. Paris saw the best in everyone, even if they were a little different.

Paris was bent over her laptop when Andrea walked into The Flower Cottage with her two boys. "Andy and Charlie are so tall. What are you feeding them?"

"Anything and everything," Andrea said with a grin. "I called in to see you at lunchtime, but you were busy with some customers."

"It's been a hectic day. I've booked another five events over the next couple of months. The social media posts Emma helped me with are really working."

"I'm glad. Remember to let me know if you need any help. I enjoyed helping you with the Kingston's wedding. Have you heard anything from your mom?"

"No, and I don't expect to. Pastor John told me he spoke to her before she left. Mom took the name and contact details of the counselor he recommended in Santa Fe. Hopefully, she makes an appointment with them."

"I hope so, too. And now," she looked at Andy and Charlie. "Drumroll please, boys."

Her sons grinned and tapped their hands on the sales counter.

"We have some exciting news that's guaranteed to make you smile. The loans officer from the bank sent me an email. She's approved my application for money to open a café in Anchor Lane!"

"That's wonderful!" Paris rushed around the counter and hugged her friend. "I'm so happy for you."

"It will be a big adjustment, but I'm looking forward to it. Do you want to come with Jackie, Shelley, and me on Friday night to celebrate? Kylie said she'll look after our children as long as we bring her some dessert."

"She's brave."

"I think she's looking forward to feeling needed. Ben has been making sure she's not overdoing things. Which means she's confined to their living room with a book or the TV remote."

Paris laughed. "Am I supposed to feel sorry for her?"

"That's what I said, too." She put her hands over Charlie's ears. "Who wouldn't want a tall, dark, handsome man waiting on them?"

"Oh, Mom," Andy said.

"A man who knows how to look after a woman is worth his weight in gold," Andrea told her son. "So, what do you say, Paris? Does a night at the Bar and Grill in downtown Sapphire Bay sound like a good idea?"

"It sounds perfect. I'll let Richard know my social calendar is filling up fast."

"How is Mr. Tall, Dark, and Handsome?"

"He's doing great. You should go and see him. He's next door in your cottage at the moment."

Andrea grinned. "Do you think he'd mind?"

"He'd love to show you and the boys around."

"In that case, we're going exploring. I'll call you tomorrow once I've booked a table at the restaurant."

"I'll look forward to hearing from you. What are you going to call your café?"

"We've decided to call it The Starlight Café."

"That's lovely. Just hearing the name makes me feel warm and cozy."

"And, hopefully, wanting a large mug of hot chocolate and lots of muffins and gourmet sandwiches."

"I definitely wouldn't say no to any of those things. Enjoy looking around your new café."

"We will."

After Andrea and the boys left, Paris went back to her laptop. Designing an over-the-top series of flower arrangements for a wedding was why she'd started her business. With a budget of astronomical proportions, and a bride and groom who were open to any ideas she might have, it was a match made in heaven.

RICHARD GROANED. Tonight's poker game wasn't going to plan. In fact, he was playing so badly that he doubted he even had a plan anymore. "That makes four losses in a row. You've cleaned me out of chips."

Wyatt rubbed his hands together. "It makes up for all the times you've made me go home with empty pockets. At the rate I'm going, I'll be able to buy Penny the new circular saw she wants for her birthday."

Ben's eyebrows rose. "You're buying your wife a power tool? Isn't there something else she wants?"

"Nope. Penny's got her heart set on the latest Bosch design. What can I say? She's a woman who knows what she wants."

"Aren't they all," Ethan grumbled. "Diana's taking me to the animal shelter on Saturday. She's seen a dog she likes, and it's all Richard's fault."

"Mine? How do you figure that?"

"After she saw Louie, my days of only having one dog in the house disappeared. Even Charlie looks at me with his big, doggy eyes, pleading for a playmate. We have until Sunday morning to decide whether we're adopting o zo."

Wyatt laughed. "Gonzo?"

"Yeah, I know. The name might have to change, but Diana's decision won't. He'll be coming home with us."

John handed Richard a can of soda. "See what you've started? Before you know it, we'll all be adopting pets from the animal shelter."

"Think of it as a new experience."

Ben grinned. "I don't need any more of those."

Richard cleared his throat. He didn't know how his friends would react to the questions he had for them, but it didn't matter. He was on a mission and only someone who'd been there before could understand how stressed he was. "I'm doing some research and I need your help."

"I hope you're not going to mention anything about work," Ethan said.

"Or anything to do with The Welcome Center, the church, or the tiny home village," John added. "If we talk about any of those things, my brain will click back into work mode."

Wyatt frowned. "Well, that cuts out most of the things Richard's involved in. If you have questions about your outdoor furniture, I'd be happy to test any new models. Your furniture should win a design award, it's so good."

"My questions don't have anything to do with any of those things, although I appreciate the comments about my furniture."

Ethan frowned. "You'd better tell us what you need before John eats all the French fries."

"What can I say," John said as he dipped another one into the ketchup. "Shelley's on a diet. This is the closest I've been to anything deep fried in weeks. I'm having withdrawal symptoms."

Richard looked around the table at the men who'd changed his life forever.

"I know that look," Ethan said suspiciously. "You're about to get all emotional and tell us how amazing we are."

"I have a box of tissues, somewhere," John said unhelpfully.

"Would you guys quit making jokes? I'm trying to be serious."

Wyatt's eyes narrowed. "You're stalling for time, that's what you're doing. It's just as well my winning streak will override any shady psychological advantage you think you're getting."

Ben laughed. "They're big words for a Friday night."

"I'm extending my vocabulary. Penny said it keeps your brain active as you age."

Richard groaned. "I don't care about your wives eating habits or your brain function. I want to ask Paris to marry me, and I don't know how."

Everyone stared at him as if he'd announced a little green man had landed in his backyard.

John was the first to recover. "I found the words 'will you marry me' worked well."

Ben covered his mouth with his hand and gave a suspicious cough.

"Don't laugh. It isn't funny," Richard told him.

Ethan rose from his chair and hugged Richard. "Paris is a great person."

After everyone had congratulated him, Richard's stress levels halved. This was the first time he'd told anyone he wanted to marry Paris. Even his conversation with Jack had been more general than specific.

Wyatt frowned. "Why are you worried about asking her to marry you? Do you think she'll say no?"

"Anything's possible, but I don't think she'll say no. At least, I hope she doesn't say no. Jack adores her, Louie sulks when she leaves our house, and I can't imagine my life without her."

"And there's your proposal," John said. "Add on the bit about asking her to marry you and you're all set."

Ben's eyes widened. "It's not only the words, is it? You want the sky to explode in fireworks and a string quartet to play soft romantic music. You want an amazing memory Paris will treasure for the rest of her life."

"That's exactly what I want." At least one of his friends understood the dilemma he was in. "But I need ideas. You guys have been through this before, but I wasn't here when most of you became engaged. What did you do?"

John sighed. "I asked Shelley to marry me on Christmas

Day in front of the tree we decorate at the end of Main Street."

"In the middle of a blizzard," Ethan laughed.

"No one noticed the temperature after Shelley said yes. Tell Richard how you proposed."

Ethan cleared his throat. "I drove Diana to Polson where the steamboats dock against the jetty. I asked her to marry me under a tree decorated in fairy lights. After she said yes, our families and friends went on an evening dinner cruise on the lake."

Richard's eyes widened. "I never thought of that."

"I stuck closer to him," Ben said next. "I blindfolded Kylie and took her to a thirty-foot Christmas tree I'd decorated on the farm."

"And you know where I was," Wyatt said to Richard. "I asked Penny to marry me in The Lakeside Inn on the day the Bed and Breakfast opened."

John must have seen the near panic on Richard's face. "You don't need fireworks and symphony orchestras. Just think of a place or memory that's special to both of you."

"Does a Harley motorcycle count?"

"It does if it's mine," Ethan said with a chuckle. "But it's supposed to be special for *both* of you."

"Or all three of us," Richard added. "Jack is an important part of my proposal."

"I've got it," Wyatt said with a slightly worrying smile. "Build a castle from giant Legos bricks. Stand inside it with Paris when you ask her to marry you. Jack will think it's the coolest thing ever."

"I'm not sure Paris would agree," Richard said. But they would remember it for the rest of their lives.

CHAPTER 22

*J*ackie raised her glass in a toast. "To Andrea. The latest business owner to join the incredible redevelopment of Anchor Lane. May your café provide endless cups of coffee, food that draws people from far and wide, and a bowl of water for our canine buddies."

Paris clinked her glass of orange juice against her friends' and smiled. After the stressful week she'd had, she was glad Andrea had suggested going out. The Bar and Grill in downtown Sapphire Bay was everything she needed to soothe her soul.

With its jukebox pumping out country hits, soft, mellow lighting making everyone look glamorous, and a mix of cowboys, business people, and retirees enjoying themselves, it was ten times better than being at home on her own.

"I can't believe I'm finally going to own a café." Andrea's face lit with happiness. "Andy and Charlie are so excited. All they've talked about is inviting their friends to the café to show them where their mom works."

"What did you think of the remodeling?" Paris asked.

Shelley and Jackie leaned forward to hear what Andrea said.

"It's gorgeous. Richard and his team are so clever. They've stopped working on the kitchen until I've decided what appliances I'm buying and where they'll go. The rest of the cottage is well on its way to being painted."

"What color have you settled on?" Shelley asked.

"I like what Paris did to The Flower Cottage, except instead of a navy blue feature wall, I thought I'd use a soft pink paint. As well as being my favorite color, it's supposed to be soothing. If it makes people stay longer in the café, I'll give anything a go." She pulled out her phone and showed a picture to everyone. "This is what inspired me."

Paris loved what she saw. A pale pink wall was the backdrop to large gold-framed mirrors. White round tables sat in front of the wall, surrounded by cane chairs and vases full of deep pink flowers. "It's gorgeous. You'll love going into work each day with a café that looks like that."

"I thought the same thing. And if I enjoy it, so will my customers."

Shelley checked her cell phone and frowned.

"Is everything okay?" Paris asked.

"It's only John. He's lost his third poker game in a row and he wants my sympathy."

Andrea grinned. "What will you tell him?"

"Nothing." Shelley raised her glass to her friends. "I'm here to enjoy your company. John will bounce back from his disappointment."

"Richard will console him. He hasn't won anything, either."

"What is it with men?" Jackie asked. "When everything's going well, you never hear from them. As soon as something goes wrong, they want all the sympathy they can get."

"That sounds like it's coming from a woman who's had her heart broken once too often."

"Do I sound that bad?"

Paris nodded and smiled. "You're in good company. Before I met Richard, I dated a few men who were like that. Richard's different. He didn't send me a text to get my sympathy, he sent it to make me laugh. I joked about losing his life savings to his friends, one dollar at a time."

"Some men, like my husband, want to tell you every little thing that's happening in their lives," Shelley added. "I love that John is so open with me. But I've developed incredibly selective hearing and choose when I look at my phone. If he wants my undivided attention straightaway, he has to bring me a bag of chocolate fudge."

"I like that idea." Andrea lifted a slice of pizza off the plate in the middle of the table. "Talking about men, how's your budding romance going, Paris?"

A blush skimmed her cheeks when her friends turned to her. "It's great."

"That's it?" Jackie asked.

"What else do you want to know?"

"Anything and everything," Andrea replied. "I'm thirty-three, single, and have two boys. My social life revolves around sports practices, after-school programs, and food."

Paris grinned. "You love your boys and you don't mind being their personal taxi service and chef."

"I know, but it's nice knowing other people have a more balanced life."

"I'm not sure my life is balanced, but I'm enjoying myself. Richard is amazing. Jack makes me laugh, and Louie is adorable."

Jackie helped herself to a slice of pizza. "It sounds like someone has been bitten by the love bug."

Shelley sighed. "I think it's wonderful you're so happy."

"I do, too," Paris said softly. "I can't imagine my life without Richard beside me."

"That's so lovely," Jackie said.

Andrea picked up her wine glass. "I'd like to propose another toast. To Paris. For finding the courage to open her heart and find true love."

A man banged into the back of Andrea's chair. Her drink flew out of her hands, landing in the middle of the table. In the pizza.

"I'm so sorry." The man grabbed their spare napkins and mopped up the wine. "I wasn't watching where I was going. I'll buy you another drink and replace the pizza."

Andrea took the napkin Jackie gave her and wiped the front of her sweater. "Don't worry. We'd eaten most of the pizza." She lifted her face to the stranger and her smile disappeared. She looked as though she'd been struck by lightning and the man didn't seem much better.

"Can I buy you something else instead?" he asked.

"We'll be okay. But thanks, anyway."

He nodded and collected the wet napkins. "I'll get rid of these."

Paris grabbed the plate holding the soggy pizza. "Put them on here. I'll take everything across to the bar."

The man dropped them onto the plate and sent an apologetic look to everyone. "I hope you enjoy the rest of your evening."

Andrea cleared her throat. "We will."

As soon as he was gone, Jackie placed her hand on Andrea's forehead. "I'm checking you're okay. That man was the most gorgeous male in the room and you didn't ask him who he was."

A blush scorched Andrea's cheeks. "I was too busy wiping my sweater to notice."

Paris stood and collected the last of the napkins. "I'll be

right back. Don't say anything about him until I return." While she was at the counter, she'd order four slices of apple pie and ask if anyone knew who the stranger was. Sapphire Bay was a small town. Someone must know who he was. And once she knew his name, she'd tell Andrea.

TWO WEEKS LATER...

RICHARD HELD the treasure-hunting bucket Jack had bought from the general store. The sapphires they'd found in Flathead Lake were genuine. The tiny gemstones were worth one hundred dollars, more than enough to buy the Legos Jack wanted.

But, instead of going straight to the toy store in Polson, he'd given half the money to John to buy food parcels for the people in the tiny home village. The other fifty dollars would eventually go toward the latest Legos model.

"I found one!" Jack hurried back to Richard and dropped the tiny, peanut-sized rock in the bucket. "That's six sapphires. How much money will the man give us for those ones?"

Richard compared the size of the stones to the ones they'd taken into the jeweler last week. "Maybe eighty dollars."

Jack grinned. "I'll find two more."

They walked to the edge of the lake. Louie was jumping in and out of the water. When he'd had enough of that, he sat on the trail, basking in the afternoon sunshine.

For the last week, Richard had wanted to talk to Jack about Paris. If his son didn't want her living permanently with them, he wouldn't ask her to marry him. They would be like the three musketeers—all for one and one for all. And if Jack wasn't happy, it wouldn't work.

"Can you see any gemstones in the water, Dad?"

Bending down, he ran his hand under the water, looking for anything that looked out of place. "Not yet. Can I ask you something?"

"Sure."

"Have you ever wondered what it would be like to have another person live with us? Someone who's like a mom?"

"Like Grandma?"

"Not like Grandma. More like my wife and your stepmom."

"Don't you like Paris anymore?"

Richard blinked. "Why did you ask me that?"

"You can't have a wife if you're dating Paris. Charlie's dad had lots of girlfriends when he was married to Charlie's mom. After that, they got a divorce. Charlie said it was scary when he came here with his mom and brother."

"I bet it was. I love Paris, and I don't want to date anyone else. I was thinking of asking her to marry me. If she says yes, she'll live with us and we'll be a family."

"Would she be my mom?"

"If you want her to, she could be."

"Okay."

"Okay?" Richard was surprised it was that easy.

"She makes pretty flowers and yummy pancakes. She knows how to bath Louie and doesn't mind when he digs holes in her garden." Jack dropped another gemstone into the bucket. "Grandma said one day you might find someone who makes you as happy as I do. When that happens, it doesn't mean you love me less. You'll just have a bigger heart that's full of love for everyone."

Richard studied Jack's solemn face. "When did Grandma tell you that?"

"Ages ago."

"How do you feel about my heart being big enough for you and Paris?"

"Good. Grandma said your heart will get even bigger if you have a baby. Can we have a kitten instead? Pastor John said there are lots at the animal shelter."

Richard hugged Jack. He'd have to thank his mom later. "I'll think about the kitten. Thank you for wanting Paris to be part of our lives."

"That's okay. If she's my mom, can I still go to her flower arranging classes?"

"You can go to as many as you like."

Jack breathed a sigh of relief.

"Would you be able to keep what we've talked about a secret? I want Paris to be surprised when I ask her to marry me."

"Okay. Let's look for more gemstones. I promised Nora I'd give her some."

Richard looked along the shore and chose a spot a few feet from where they were standing. Over the last two weeks, he'd had a chance to think about how he would propose to Paris. He had a location, hundreds of fairy lights, and the words he wanted to say. All he needed was a ring, and for Paris to say yes.

CHAPTER 23

 WEEK LATER...

JOHN LEANED sideways on the ladder. "Throw the lights this way."

Richard hoisted the rope of fairy lights into the air, hoping they landed close to where John was pointing. Decorating the apple tree in his backyard was more of a mission than he realized. The fairy lights snagged on the branches, making them almost impossible to move.

Richard's mom opened the back door and walked toward them. "It's looking good. How will you know if you've covered the entire tree? It will be too late to add more lights once it's dark."

"We're crossing our fingers and sending a special message to the man upstairs," John said as he stepped onto the next rung of the ladder. "It will be a miracle if I go home in one piece. I've almost fallen twice."

Richard looked around the yard. "Hey, Ethan. Can you

stand at the bottom of the ladder and make sure John's okay?"

"No problem. I'll be there soon."

Over the last few weeks, Richard had replaced the rickety old fence surrounding the property with a straight, white picket fence. Ethan was adding a trailer-load of flower-shaped lights to the fence. Hopefully, they turned out as impressive as the picture they'd seen on the Internet.

Louie hopped across the backyard with a stick in his mouth.

Jack chased after him. "It's called fetch, Louie. You're supposed to give me the stick."

There wasn't much hope of that. After a month of dog training, Louie was still getting used to some commands.

"Be careful around the ladder," Richard told his son.

"Okay." Jack wrestled the stick from Louie and stared at the tree. "Why are you putting lights in the tree?"

"To make it look pretty."

"Will Paris like it more?"

"I hope so."

Richard's mom stood beside them. "There's fresh lemonade and cookies in the kitchen if you want a snack."

A rustle from high in the tree made them all look up. "That was perfect timing, Carol. I've finished putting the lights on the tree. All we have to do is tidy the yard and make sure Louie doesn't destroy the new garden."

"The temporary barrier should work," Ethan said as he walked toward them. "The lights around the white picket fence are ready, too."

Richard checked the time. Paris had gone to Polson with Andrea to look at some secondhand tables and chairs. On the way home, they were having dinner with Kylie and Ben at the Christmas tree farm. Ben had promised he wouldn't let them leave before nine o'clock.

His mom placed her hand on his arm. "Don't worry. It will be fine."

He opened his arms and hugged her. "You've never told me how dad proposed to you."

Carol laughed. "It wasn't nearly as romantic as what you've done. We went to the last drive-in movie in our town. At the end of the movie, your dad stood on the trunk of his car and proposed to me." She smiled at the grin on Richard's face. "We were studying Romeo and Juliet at school. I think it was his balcony moment."

"How old were you?"

"Seventeen." Carol sighed. "I can still see him standing there, full of excitement for what lay ahead of us. Time goes by quickly, so make each day count with Paris. She's a wonderful woman."

"I will. I'm glad you married Dad."

"So am I. And do you know what? I wouldn't change a moment of our lives together. You were the icing on the cake."

"Grandma! Come quick. The cookies smell like they're burning."

"Oh, dear. I left the last batch in the oven." Carol spun around and rushed toward the back door.

Richard was right behind her.

Before they made it to the house, Ethan hurried outside holding a smoking cookie sheet. "They're burned beyond redemption."

Carol took one look at the cookies and pointed to the trash can. "Out they go. It's just as well we still have plenty of others."

They went inside and threw open the kitchen windows. Richard looked around the room and sighed. He never thought he'd own a home, let alone ask someone to share his life with him and Jack. But here he was, about to ask one of the most important questions of his life, and dreading what Paris would say.

ANDREA PULLED into Richard's driveway. "I can't believe the tables and chairs were so inexpensive."

"We were lucky the seller wanted to get rid of them so quickly. They'll look gorgeous in your café." Paris unbuckled her seatbelt and stared at Richard's house. There wasn't one light on anywhere. "That's strange. I'm sure Richard said to meet him here."

"Maybe something happened. Check your cell phone."

Reaching into her bag, Paris quickly found her phone and checked her texts and emails. "Nothing."

Andrea got out of her truck. "Let's check the backyard. I can hear music."

"Jack was talking about camping outside one night this week. Maybe that's what they're doing."

"Someone must be there."

Paris looked at the neighbors' houses. At first, she'd thought there must be a power outage, but other lights were on.

"Watch where you step," Andrea said from ahead of her. "I nearly tripped over a paving stone."

Paris turned on her phone's flashlight. "Is that better?"

"Why didn't I think of that?" A few seconds later, Andrea disappeared around the edge of the house.

Her gasp made Paris rush forward. "Are you okay?" As soon as she stepped into the backyard, she froze. The apple tree was glowing with twinkling fairy lights, and the swing Jack loved was wrapped in sheer fabric and even more lights.

"Look at the fence," Andrea whispered.

Pink, purple, and red flower-shaped lights decorated the

entire yard. It was like stepping into a fantastic dream, complete with someone playing a country ballad on a guitar.

Paris looked closer at the woman whose voice sent goose bumps along her skin. "Is that Willow?"

Andrea looked across the yard and smiled. "It is."

"What's she—"

"Surprise."

Paris didn't know whether it was the softly spoken word or the hands that settled on her waist that made her jump. But she did, right into the man standing behind her.

Richard's groan filled the yard.

"I'm so sorry. Are you all right?"

Andrea peered at Richard. "I think his nose is bleeding."

Paris held up her phone and shone the flashlight onto his face.

Richard's eyes clamped shut. "I'm okay." Carefully, he touched his nose.

"It isn't bleeding." Paris put her phone away before something else happened. "Why did you sneak up on me? You nearly gave me a heart attack."

"I wanted to surprise you."

"Me?"

Richard nodded.

Andrea's eyes widened. She looked around them and cleared her throat. "I'll go and see Willow while you talk."

Paris watched her friend walk across the yard. None of this was making sense. "This is beautiful, but I don't understand why you did it. My birthday is months away."

"It isn't for your birthday." Richard wiped tears from his eyes. "You have a hard head."

"Do you want some Tylenol? I have some in my bag."

"I'll get one later. Come and have a look at the lights." Richard held her hand and led her toward the apple tree.

"This must have taken a long time to do. How did you string so many lights in the branches?"

"We had a high ladder. John and Ethan helped me."

Paris looked around the backyard. "Are they still here?"

"Not *here*, precisely."

Willow started singing again.

"Why is Willow here?" she whispered.

"Because I asked her to sing for us."

That made absolutely no sense, unless Richard was expecting more people to arrive. When she realized what was happening, she was much happier. "Having a party is a wonderful idea. Jack will love what you've done. Is he inside?"

"He's with Mom." Richard cleared his throat. With both hands holding hers, he looked into her eyes. "I decorated the backyard because I want you to remember this night for the rest of your life. You mean the world to me, Paris. I didn't realize how amazing you are until we worked together on The Flower Cottage. On the days I didn't see you, I missed you. You accept me as I am. You're kind and patient, and one of the nicest people I've ever met."

Paris' heart pounded. Richard couldn't be doing what she thought he was. When he kneeled on one knee, all her worst nightmares flared to life.

"I can't," she whispered.

Even from the glow of the fairy lights, she saw his skin turn white. "What do you mean?"

"I can't marry you."

He rose to his feet and held her hands more firmly. "You don't love me?"

"I do. I love you more than I've ever loved anyone else. I can't wait to see you each day. Even if we're watching a movie with Jack and Louie, I'm happy and content, and all the things I've never been."

"Are you worried about your stickability issue?"

Tears filled her eyes. "I don't want to ever say goodbye, but I'm worried about what will happen."

Richard breathed a sigh of relief. "What if I make you a promise?"

"Like the ones we made when we started dating?"

"Something like that. What if I promise I'll love you until the day I die? That I'll wrap my arms around you each day and tell you you're my shining star. That I'll always be here for you, through all the ups and downs of our life together." He lifted his hand to her face and wiped away her tears. "That I'll be right beside you until you're not worried about your stickability issue anymore."

Paris took a deep, trembling breath. If she walked away from Richard tonight, there would be no coming back. All the dreams she'd pushed to the back of her mind would stay there, stuck in a past she couldn't change. They'd already taken the first step toward building a life together. She could take one more, even if it was a giant leap into the unknown.

She placed her hand over his heart. "That's a wonderful promise."

"But is it enough?"

"It will always be enough. For most of my life, I've run from any form of commitment. But if I run tonight, I'll be leaving the only man who's ever made me feel whole. You understand who I am and what I need, even before I do. You're my soft place to fall and my greatest supporter. I couldn't think of anything better than spending the rest of my life with you."

"Does that mean you'll marry me?"

Paris nodded. Through her tears she saw a small, wooden box in Richard's hand. "You bought me a ring?"

"*We* bought you a ring." He held out his hand, and Jack joined them.

"Why are you crying?" Jack asked.

Paris wiped her face. "They're happy tears. How do you feel about me marrying your dad?"

"It will be fun. We can take Louie for more walks and watch *Shrek* whenever we want. Have you seen the garden we made?"

Paris looked around the yard.

"It's over here." Jack pulled her to an area that was surrounded by lavender. "There's a space in the middle for another plant."

"What kind of plant?"

Richard sent her a gentle smile. "I thought you might want to put your dad's rose there."

Fresh tears stung her eyes. "You remembered."

"I want you to be happy, and having that connection to him is important to you."

Jack tugged the sleeve of his dad's jacket. "Paris hasn't seen her ring."

"You're right." Richard held the box in front of her. "Are you ready?"

"I am." When he opened the box, her mouth dropped open.

"It's a sapphire," Jack said quickly. "Like the ones we found in the lake, but it's big and shiny."

"It's the prettiest ring I've ever seen."

For the second time that night, Richard got down on one knee. "Paris Haynes. Will you marry me and be a special part of Jack's life?"

"And Louie's," Jack whispered.

Richard smiled. "And Louie's."

Paris nodded. "I'd love to marry you and become a new family."

A loud cheer rang out from the house. Paris turned

around, surprised to see Richard's mom and their friends coming outside. "Were they hiding inside all this time?"

Richard nodded. "Mom was keeping everyone quiet."

Andrea hurried across the yard and hugged Paris. "Congratulations. Are you all right?"

"I think so. I'm feeling a little overwhelmed."

"Enjoy tonight. You can catch your breath tomorrow."

John handed Paris a glass of orange juice and Richard a glass of champagne. "I'd like to make a toast."

Everyone smiled as they held the glass they'd brought outside with them.

"Congratulations on your engagement. We're excited and humbled to be part of tonight's celebration. Enjoy your lives together and live each day to its fullest. To Paris, Richard, and Jack."

Everyone one raised their glass. "To Paris, Richard, and Jack."

And with the sound of their friends' voices carrying on the still night air, Paris and Richard celebrated their love for each other. Now and forever.

THE END

THANK YOU

Thank you for reading *The Flower Cottage* I hope you enjoyed it! If you did…

1. Help other people find this book by **writing a review.**
2. Sign up for my **new releases e-mail**, so you can find out about the next book as soon as it's available.
3. Come like my **Facebook** page.
4. Visit my website: **leeannamorgan.com**

Keep reading to enjoy an excerpt from **The Starlight Cafe**, Andrea and David's story, the second book in *The Cottages on Anchor Lane* series!

LEEANNA MORGAN

THE Starlight CAFE

The Starlight Cafe
The Cottages on Anchor Lane Series
Book Two

**Fans of Robyn Carr's Virgin River series will love this
small-town, feel-good romance!**

Andrea Smith is determined to give her two sons a happy life
in Sapphire Bay. After leaving an abusive marriage, the peace

and stability she's found in the small Montana town soothes her soul and gives her the courage to rebuild her life.

With the development of the cottages on Anchor Lane underway, she sees an opportunity to open the café she's always dreamed about. It will take a lot of hard work and more money than she has, but she needs to make this work—for her and her children.

David O'Dowd is the Clinical Director of BioTech Industries--a high-tech medical device company that's changing people's lives. With the company opening a research facility in Sapphire Bay, it's David's job to find the perfect building and keep their investors happy.

When he sees the cottages on Anchor Lane being remodeled, he's intrigued by the woman who's working day and night to open a new café. When he meets her sons, he can't help but be inspired by what she's trying to do. But with mounting costs and limited resources, Andrea needs help to fund the rest of the project.

With David's financial skills and Andrea's enthusiasm, they work together to create a future that's brighter than either of them imagined. But will their past tragedies allow them to build a new life together, or will they tear them apart?

THE STARLIGHT CAFE is the second book in *The Cottages on Anchor Lane* series and can easily be read as a stand-alone.

All of Leeanna's series are linked. If you find a character you like, they could be in another novel!

**CLICK HERE TO
PRE-ORDER YOUR COPY TODAY!**

ENJOY MORE BOOKS BY LEEANNA MORGAN

Montana Brides:

Book 1: Forever Dreams (Gracie and Trent)

Book 2: Forever in Love (Amy and Nathan)

Book 3: Forever After (Nicky and Sam)

Book 4: Forever Wishes (Erin and Jake)

Book 5: Forever Santa (A Montana Brides Christmas Novella)

Book 6: Forever Cowboy (Emily and Alex)

Book 7: Forever Together (Kate and Dan)

Book 8: Forever and a Day (Sarah and Jordan)

Montana Brides Boxed Set: Books 1-3

Montana Brides Boxed Set: Books 4-6

The Bridesmaids Club:

Book 1: All of Me (Tess and Logan)

Book 2: Loving You (Annie and Dylan)

Book 3: Head Over Heels (Sally and Todd)

Book 4: Sweet on You (Molly and Jacob)

The Bridesmaids Club: Books 1-3

Emerald Lake Billionaires:

Book 1: Sealed with a Kiss (Rachel and John)

Book 2: Playing for Keeps (Sophie and Ryan)

Book 3: Crazy Love (Holly and Daniel)

Book 4: One And Only (Elizabeth and Blake)

Emerald Lake Billionaires: Books 1-3

The Protectors:

Book 1: Safe Haven (Hayley and Tank)

Book 2: Just Breathe (Kelly and Tanner)

Book 3: Always (Mallory and Grant)

Book 4: The Promise (Ashley and Matthew)

The Protectors Boxed Set: Books 1-3

Montana Promises:

Book 1: Coming Home (Mia and Stan)

Book 2: The Gift (Hannah and Brett)

Book 3: The Wish (Claire and Jason)

Book 4: Country Love (Becky and Sean)

Montana Promises Boxed Set: Books 1-3

Sapphire Bay:

Book 1: Falling For You (Natalie and Gabe)

Book 2: Once In A Lifetime (Sam and Caleb)

Book 3: A Christmas Wish (Megan and William)

Book 4: Before Today (Brooke and Levi)

Book 5: The Sweetest Thing (Cassie and Noah)

Book 6: Sweet Surrender (Willow and Zac)

Sapphire Bay Boxed Set: Books 1-3

Sapphire Bay Boxed Set: Books 4-6

Santa's Secret Helpers:

Book 1: Christmas On Main Street (Emma and Jack)

Book 2: Mistletoe Madness (Kylie and Ben)

Book 3: Silver Bells (Bailey and Steven)

Book 4: The Santa Express (Shelley and John)

Book 5: Endless Love (The Jones Family)

Santa's Secret Helpers Boxed Set: Books 1-3

Return To Sapphire Bay:

Book 1: The Lakeside Inn (Penny and Wyatt)

Book 2: Summer At Lakeside (Diana and Ethan)

Book 3: A Lakeside Thanksgiving (Barbara and Theo)

Book 4: Christmas At Lakeside (Katie and Peter)

Return to Sapphire Bay Boxed Set (Books 1-3)

The Cottages on Anchor Lane:

Book 1: The Flower Cottage (Paris and Richard)

Book 2: The Starlight Café (Andrea and David)

Book 3: The Cozy Quilt Shop (Shona and Joseph)

Book 4: A Stitch in Time (Jackie and Aidan)